Delilah of Sunhats and Swans
a novel
by
Melissa Volker

For my father –
One, solitary black-eyed susan
You are here in these pages
And for Christopher –
Just because
And for Lex –
For the reminder

Acknowledgements:

My mother, the poet, my father and his ruthless red pen. Schmev -- I love you. Alice -- thank you for your generosity.

Excerpts from the following authors are quoted throughout:

Ralph Waldo Emerson, Emily Dickinson, George Sewell, Henry Wadsworth Longfellow, Lord Byron, John Milton, William Wordsworth, Walt Whitman, William Blake, Caroline E.S. Norton, Lewis Caroll, Dylan Thomas and William Shakespeare.

I am grateful for their words, their hearts, their spirits.

"The heart has its reasons
which reason knows nothing of."
"We know the truth, not only by reason,
but by the heart."
Blaise Pascal, Lettres Provinciales

*H*arold Reinman had an itch.

Standing on the library steps, shielded from the rain by the extended roof, he felt an odd, annoying tickle somewhere inside his skull, in his brain. It was an unreachable, impossible-to-satisfy itch –- the same one he always seemed to feel before something happened. So he waited. He waited and wondered what would happen.

From behind him it came, from back near the police station and post office, past the craft store and Millie's Milliner. It rumbled and squealed around the corner, faces peering through the dark, tinted glass streaked with rain; faces watching him watching them.

He watched the bus grind down Main Street as the itch in his brain grew more intense. He watched it pass the pharmacy that sold candy out of glass jars, pass Landers Hardware and the butcher, pass what used to be Emmett's gas station but was now an empty shack with rusted pumps, and pass Hattie's dress shop. He wondered where it was headed, his finger absently rubbing a spot on his skull, and then he remembered: Amos. The bus stops at Amos' store.

The brakes of the bus let out a high-pitched squeal, the strained whine of transition from open throttle to stillness, of a child forced to come inside before he is ready. As the door hissed open, Delilah paused at the top of the steps, listened to the "click, click" of the windshield wipers beating a seemingly syncopated rhythm to that of her heart.

"Are you getting off here or not?" the driver asked, his words verbal prodding she could feel in the small of her back.

That was the question she now asked herself, '*Am I getting off here?*'

For days she had watched highways pass, sucked beneath the bus' front bumper and spit out the rear window while time vanished in a blur of roadsides and white lines, the endless rumble occasionally interrupted by the hypnotic hum of tires against grooves cut into the road. She grew mindless watching.

Gears grinding, belching exhaust, the bus had roared through backwater towns where children idled in muddy front yards behind rusting fences—a girl with her finger in her nose, a boy drawing pictures in the dirt with a stick, others sitting solemnly on steps and curbs, popsicle juice running colored tracks to their elbows so if they stood together, arm to arm, they'd make a faint, murky rainbow. She stared out at old women with blue hair and brown orthopedic shoes sitting on benches along local routes, gazes distant, full of longing; at women pushing strollers through pedestrian crosswalks, babies lolling in oblivious slumber; then highways and more highways, all speeding by, bleeding together in the world beyond the tinted windows. She'd watched it all through sleepy and curious eyes.

"Hey, c'mon -- are you getting off or not?" The driver asked again, his voice suddenly distorted in her ears like a recording played too slowly. She felt her heart beat -- once, twice -- and the answer came not as a string of certain logic, but as an instinctive, resounding "yes" that prompted Delilah to take the steps down and out into the steady rain. She glanced up, the northeast, spring sky so low with angry black clouds that people walked with their shoulders hunched and heads bowed for fear they'd collide with the belly of the storm.

She watched vicious gusts of wind tear at umbrellas, raking at them as though full of a personal vendetta that left skeletal carcasses of bent metal and torn nylon discarded in garbage cans.

People ran for cover, ducking into shops and under awnings or inside the combination quickmart and lunch counter where conversation paused, heads turned toward the window to take note of the newcomer as she stood in the muddy drive.

The backpack over her left shoulder, her left hand holding a brown paper bag that quickly grew dark and wet in the downpour, she stood a moment, as those inside returned to their lunches and the bus ground into gear and hissed back onto the road. Cascading rivulets caught around the hood of her sweatshirt, dripped from her fingertips, turned her faded blue jeans deep indigo. As a child she was often left alone with no one to chastise her for running out into the summer rain, soaking her dress, her shoes, arms outstretched in delightful acceptance of the refreshing wash of water that soaked her to the bone. It was a pleasure she never outgrew.

When she finally stepped through the door of the quickmart, her long, copper ringlets of hair already dripping, her paper bag abruptly gave up the ghost, spilling its contents onto the tile floor where a puddle had already begun to form around her.

Again, heads turned toward her as she wiped the rain from her eyes, her hair off her face, and glanced down at the pile of her insignificant belongings -- a few books, a brush, her bus ticket. She felt several pairs of eyes on her as she sighed, met the gaze of the man behind the counter, and asked, "Would you have an extra bag I could have? Perhaps a plastic one so that I don't have a recurrence of this little mess?" Then she smiled, as beyond the windows tentative sunshine suddenly glowed faintly through thinning cloud cover and winked off remaining raindrops as they slid from leaves and awnings.

The man smiled in return, grabbed a bag from beside the cash register and moved toward her extending his hand. "I think I can spare one. My name is Amos Harrison, by the way. And you are currently puddling the floor of my store." He laughed.

"I'm sorry." She took the bag from him, pausing to notice his eyes, how their deep, mahogany color nearly matched the rich, dark complexion of his skin. He was taller than she first thought, and although his navy t-shirt pulled tightly across his expanding girth, he did not move like a man heavy with excess weight, but rather like a man who is comfortably solid in stature. "Delilah. I'm Delilah."

$\mathcal{M}$oments before Delilah stepped off the bus, Amos had just finished a conversation about how life's unpredictable nature could sometimes produce pleasant surprises. How sometimes, particularly recently, he needed that kind of reminder and that occasionally life had an uncanny way of answering a need.

He wondered if that conversation was what prompted him to invite Delilah to sit at his counter, or was it simply that she was soaked with rain and smiled at him like she had missed him terribly although they'd only just met.

Amos watched as Delilah, having placed all her clothes in the bag he'd given her, looked uncertain about what to do next. She wiped her eyes and rubbed her mouth, then looked behind her as though she had forgotten something. She started to gather her things like she was going to leave.

"Why don't you give me that sweatshirt?" Amos took Delilah's bags and set them near a counter stool. "I'll hang it in the kitchen to dry off."

"Um — well, okay. Thanks." Delilah slipped off the sweatshirt and handed it to him. The shirt beneath it was damp, but wearable.

"Sit down. I'll be right back." Amos went around the counter toward the kitchen.

Delilah slid onto the stool, avoiding the inquisitive glances from other patrons. She pulled several napkins from the holder to dry her face and catch the drips from her hair.

When Amos returned he handed her a towel. "For your hair," he said, and set a cup coffee in front of her.

"Oh — thanks again." She spun away from the counter and tipped her head to the side, catching her hair in the towel and squeezing out the excess water.

"How about some soup?" He set out silverware for her.

Delilah paused, her mouth dropping open, her eyes darting to his for a moment before looking away. She started to reach for one of her bags, changed her mind, took a breath. "Oh, that's okay. Thanks. I'm really not very hungry."

Amos hesitated, then leaned on the counter. "If it's money you're worried about, forget it. Besides, it wasn't really a question. See, I have this rule that everyone has to have a bowl of soup the first time they sit at my counter."

Delilah half-smiled. "It's a rule, huh?"

"Yup."

"Well, I wouldn't want to start out by breaking any rules."

Amos smiled. "Good." He tapped the window counter and signaled Skeet, his part-time cook, to fill a bowl.

A moment passed as Amos watched Delilah towel her hair. He sensed that she hadn't stopped here on purpose, but beyond that he had no guesses.

"So—Delilah is a beautiful name."

"Oh, thank you. I want to say it was my grandmother's." Draping the towel over her shoulders she spooned two sugars into her coffee and sipped at it.

"You *want* to say?"

"Yeah—well—I'm not sure if it's something someone actually told me once, or if I made it up myself somewhere along the line." She glanced directly up at him. The first time she'd done that.

Her gaze connected so sharply it actually made Amos jump. Like the deer he'd stumbled across in the woods as a child, the way the doe snapped her gaze to him and froze. His heart skipped a beat then as well.

"You know what I mean?" Delilah asked.

Amos ran his hand over his chin and shook his head. "Yup. Yup, I do. But that sort of confusion isn't supposed to happen until you get old."

"Now, who told you that?" Delilah folded her arms in mock derision. "I'm afraid you been misled. That kind of confusion can strike at any time! Well, that kind and others, frankly."

"How old are you?" Amos challenged.

"Eighteen," she answered, bringing the coffee to her lips again and eyeing Amos over the rim of the mug.

In that gaze, the glance that shot up to him from beneath long, pale lashes, Amos saw something far older than only eighteen years. Something juxtaposed with her playful smile. Something he felt she could no more shake or disregard than she could disown her shadow. It did not cloud her smile, or hinder it in any way, it merely colored it with something richer. Something deeper. Something beautiful and dark and unsettling.

"Why?"

"Hm?" Amos was pulled from thought.

"Why did you want to know my age?"

"Just curious."

"Ah, well — I'll caution you there. We all know about curiosity and the cat."

Amos cocked his eyebrow. "I could be killed for asking your age?"

"The world is a strange place, Mr. Harrison."

"Amos. Please."

"Amos."

Amos chuckled. She was endearing, this girl.

"And may I now inquire as to your age? I mean, fair is fair."

"I'm forty-eight." Noticing her coffee cup was empty he turned to the kitchen and retrieved the bowl of soup.

"Hrm." Delilah pushed the coffee cup out of the way.

"What?" Amos brought the soup and set it in front of her, watching her close her eyes and inhale the rising steam. It made him think she hadn't had a good meal in a while.

"Nothing." She shrugged and picked up a spoon.

"You said, 'hrm'." He retrieved a tuna sandwich from the window and placed that beside the bowl of soup.

"Yes I did."

"What did you mean by it?" He pouted, knitting his brow and looking hurt.

Delilah shook her head. "Nothing." She dunked the spoon in the soup and smiled self-consciously.

"Oh please." Amos rolled his eyes. "Women *never* mean nothing when they say 'hrm'."

"Really? What *do* they mean?" She set down the spoon, folded her arms on the table and gave Amos her full attention. She dared to admit she was enjoying herself. She hadn't spoken to anyone at length in a long while.

"Well –- I don't know." He scratched his head, tugged at his ear, and slid his hands into his pockets.

"Oh. Then I'll tell you." But she sat silently. Waiting.

Amos shrugged. "Well?"

Delilah glanced around her. "It's a very big secret. You must swear never to reveal it."

"Oh, I swear." Amos raised his hand in promise.

Delilah leaned in, motioning Amos to do the same. "It means..." she glanced around again, drawing Amos in, and whispered, "Nothing."

Amos stood back and laughed, waving her away. And watching her, he noticed how behind the laughter full of bells and breezes, she looked nearly ready to cry.

Again, as if her eyes and the rest of her were not connected, belonging to two separate people.

There was something about her, the sheer luminosity of her ivory complexion that seemed made of porcelain, dappled with just the barest hint of freckles; her impossibly small, delicately planned nose, and her loopy mane of hair the color of an autumn sunset, bright as copper wire, and her mottled, shining, almond-shaped hazel eyes, so full of something larger than her frail, lanky, eighteen year old frame should be able to carry.

Or if not the individual parts, then the sum of them together—*something* about her made him want to laugh, or cry, made him lightheaded and sad, filled him with a simple quietness that spoke more words than he would know in a lifetime. It disarmed him, made him feel heavier and more earthbound than usual. While she just sat there sipping coffee, and smiling.

The lunch crowd became demanding, pulling Amos' attention away from her, so Delilah hunched over her steaming bowl of soup while watching Amos take care of other patrons. She ignored the occasional hushed whispers and glances in her direction, all of which she saw Amos deflect simply with a wave of his hand, a quick response, and a smile in her direction.

Someone at the other end of the counter said something she couldn't hear that caused Amos to toss his head back in reverberating laughter that seemed to rumble up from somewhere around his knees. Hearing it made her laugh softly to herself as well. She watched as he refilled mugs with coffee, his small impish eyes alive with silent laughter, the gentle lines and furrows of his face like soft wrinkles in velvet, and she was reminded of an over-sized teddy bear, lumbering and heavy but soft and full of tenderness. It stirred remembrances numbed and forgotten by time and neglect.

From somewhere in her childhood came a memory of a cold, clear winter night, her small body enveloped in a soft, plush quilt, her mother's arms wrapped around her as they sat in the quiet darkness, her mother whispering lines of poetry, watching the confetti flakes of snow tumble past the window. She recalled the soft scent of lilies –- perfume? –- and the powdered aroma of the quilt as she buried her nose in its warmth.

She was so tired. Sitting on that stool, the sun through the window now warming her, muttering voices around her, the smell of the soup. She felt she could just shut her eyes and sleep. Sleep forever.

"So, Delilah? What brings you to our little town?" A woman with dark, bobbed hair and a tailored, manicured style out of place amid the cotton plaids and denim around her, appeared on the stool beside Delilah, startling her. "Just passing through? Where to? Have you traveled far? Those two bags aren't all of your things, are they?" But before she could even consider answering, Amos intervened.

"Millie. Please. Don't overwhelm the girl." He turned toward Delilah. "This is Millie Attison, our resident style consultant and entrepreneur. She owns a hat shop around the corner on Stafford Street."

"I didn't know there still *were* any hat shops anywhere." Delilah said between spoonfuls.

"Well, not only does one exist," Millie answered, "but for some reason the women in this town are nuts for it. I swear, every one of them must own at least a half dozen hats if not more. And they keep buying them! I rarely see them actually wearing them, mind you. They just buy them."

Delilah was struck by an image of houses full of hats; on doorknobs and mirror corners, hooks and chairs.

Amos interjected before Delilah was overcome by Millie's growing monologue. "Millie makes all her own hats, and if she isn't careful she'll put our quiet little town on the map." He paused, glancing at Millie. "In fact, Millie, weren't you just saying you were thinking of hiring some help? I mean, now that you've got orders coming from New York City and all."

Millie looked from Delilah to Amos and back again. "Does that mean you plan to stay on here?"

Delilah kept her gaze on her soup bowl, on the navy stripe that ran around the rim, prodding bits of potato and lima bean with her spoon, remembering the truth of her life, the reason she was in this town, at this place, at this moment. Deep in her temples a dull pain gestated. Her breath sounded loud in her ears, the voices of those around her dulled to a muted hum. "I—I hadn't really thought about it, I guess." Her voice rang tinny in her ear, as though she spoke into a can as her mind whirred silently around on itself. Before the question was, *Are you getting off here?* Now it was, *Are you staying?* But there were no real plans. No certainties. Until an hour ago there had been only highway, vague possibilities, and pervasive sadness. Like a leaf caught in a river current

13

she had drifted from town to town pausing at those whose names she liked, this one possessing a ring softer and gentler than any other. How many times had she considered stopping? How many times had she gotten back on the bus? How long could that pattern continue?

Amos' suspicion that this girl was currently without a home or a plan solidified as he watched her struggle. The creature that owned her eyes took hold and transformed the rest of her. He watched the parade of thoughts pass through those eyes and slid a piece of warm apple pie on the counter in front of her, compelled to soften the ache he saw there. "Maybe you should." Sometimes a lost soul needed a signpost, someone or something to suggest an answer. Even a temporary one.

From beneath a damp curl of hair Delilah breathed in the cinnamon and spices and glanced from the pie to Amos, who stood with his arms folded loosely across his chest, his brows raised teasingly. She cleared her throat, which had suddenly gone dry. "Maybe I will." She felt as though she teetered on a precipice, the next step heart-wrenching but inevitable. To begin anew one must completely step out of the old. And isn't that what she wanted?

"You should." Placing a fork on the edge of the plate Amos nudged the pie closer to her, his eyes dancing. "What if I throw in some vanilla ice cream?" In the back of his mind he briefly wondered why it seemed to matter to him — whether or not this girl remained — but just as quickly as the thought came, it left.

She smiled in spite of herself, the whirring in her brain ebbing away. "Chocolate chip?"

"You got it."

"Okay." She spoke the words on a puff of air, forcing them clear before she could swallow them and pulled the pie toward her.

Stepping off the edge, what she had thought to be empty void, actually held safe, solid ground.

Millie, suddenly feeling like she had missed some silent communication spoke up, "What?"

Delilah kept her gaze on Amos as she lift a forkful of steaming apple pie from the plate. "I'll stay." Instantly the weight of miles of empty road and weeks of vagueness slipped from her shoulders.

Amos leaned back against the wall behind the counter and smiled. "Welcome to Macaenas."

Upon her decision to stay Amos directed Delilah to Virginia Emmett's place on Ellington Street, next door to his own house. She had a room for rent.

Following Amos' directions to Virginia's, Delilah turned left outside his store and walked east on Main Street. Pausing once to glance back at the store, a whitewashed, clapboard structure complete with soda and ice machine on one side of the front door and a green, wrought-iron bench on the other, she experienced a moment of powerful melancholy—an unexplainable feeling of homecoming. She fought a moment with a feeling that nothing comes for free, that this instant acceptance she was experiencing would eventually demand payment. Then she bit her lip and forced the thought down and out, knowing she needed to just believe. To get where she wanted to be was going to take at least a little faith.

Eighteen years may not be long in terms of time on this earth, but it's plenty of time to become lost, by choice, accident, or circumstance.

Now, what she left behind when stepping off the bus—anger, fear, a fairytale ogre come to life—disappeared at a distant vanishing point, leaving only the street on which she stood. Ground as familiar as any. And steadier than most. For the first time in a long while she admitted to herself that she was glad for a chance to stop. Just stop.

Swallowing the lump she felt in her throat and taking a steadying breath, she glanced around her at a town cradled in a small valley between rolling foothills; dense, northern woods full of birch, silver maple and poplar, dogwood and crabapple and oak. She imagined that come autumn those woods would vibrantly transform, setting the hills aflame. And in winter, when pristine snow blanketed the ground, the branches would become bare and encased in ice as a cold fog settled along the valley floor all white and misty, making everything look eerie and magical and made of glass.

Adjusting her backpack she continued on, past a small Laundromat, a florist, and a newsstand, where an older man outside arranging newspapers waved to her as though he saw her pass by every afternoon.

She smiled.

Amos took a break and stepped outside. The air smelled of damp earth and pine. Harold Reinman sat on

16

the bench drinking an orange soda and staring at his sneakers, laces dragging in a puddle. Amos sat quietly beside him and looked out at Main street and the hills beyond, trying to see it all through a newcomer's eyes.

Macaenas was the quintessential idyllic town. Massive, gnarled oaks, trunks so wide it took four adults holding hands to reach all the way around were common; the town carefully built around them. It seemed possible that their roots might have intertwined beneath the earth forming a complex and sturdy base upon which the town comfortably rested like a baby in its mother's arms.

Of those who lived there, most had families that went back a generation or two. Few ever left. Many who did returned later in life to soothe the wounds of a harsher world beyond the town limits. Others arrived from uneventful pasts, finally looking up to find themselves in a seemingly forgotten town, and falling into its rhythms as though they'd been there their whole lives.

Faces had names, names had lives, lives had histories — and futures.

It was a small, New England town.

One you wouldn't notice, or find, except by accident.

It almost seemed the folks who built the town and those who made their lives here had planned it that way. By the time someone noticed it, they were already through it, and rarely ever thought to turn back.

So Delilah's appearance created a momentary stir in their serene existence like a pebble tossed into the still waters of a pond.

"So Amos..." Sarah Martinson stepped outside.

"Hello, Sarah. How's the craft business?" Amos spoke without looking at her. He was still studying the landscape.

Sarah moved toward the bench. "You know I'm not out here to talk about arts and crafts."

Amos squinted up at her, the sun glaring behind her. "What *are* you here to talk about?" He feigned ignorance.

"Okay, fine. If you want to be that way, who is she?"

"I don't know. Delilah is her name."

"Delilah what? Where is she from? Does she have family here or something?"

Amos was distracted by the way Sarah's eyebrows moved when she spoke, like they had a life of their own. They were also several shades darker than the flaxen blonde of her hair, which she always wore in loose, tousled curls. *Earth Woman*, was how Amos thought of her.

Millie stepped outside during Sarah's last run of questions and moved toward them both. "Forget it, Sarah. He doesn't know anything. Or if he does, he's not sharing." She looked at Amos out of the corner of her eye. "I'm very hurt." She smiled and slapped him playfully on the arm.

Amos smiled and shook his head. "All I know is that she's eighteen, probably a little lost, does not appear to be an outpatient or a convict -- "

"And has a smile that'd melt butter," Millie interjected

Amos laughed. "Okay. That's enough. She needed a place to stay so I told her to see Virginia."

It was Sarah's turn to shake her head and smile. "You and Virginia. I bet when you two were kids you both had a houseful of strays."

"There are worse things." Amos said, waving to them both as they walked away.

Delilah turned onto Ellington Street and saw the Emmett house as Amos had described it. A peach-colored Victorian with soft, white shutters, carved porch railings, and small, half-circles of stained glass capping tall, slender windows; it was almost a gingerbread house of storybook Christmases. Its sweeping porch was open and welcoming, radiating warmth, whispering soft, tantalizing invitations. As Delilah's gaze shifted to the reaching arms of elm trees whose sheltering leaves swept the eave of the roof, then slid down to the crocuses and daffodils planted around the front yard, bright and colorful, she dared to hope she may have found something of what she was looking for. It filled her, this home, this—possibility—and for a moment it had the glow of fairytales.

From her wicker rocker on the large front porch where she'd watched the rain earlier, Virginia now watched someone walk toward the house. She knew right away that the girl was looking for her, knew she was looking to stay. It was more than the backpack and the tired gait — Virginia could see a need in the stranger. A need she knew she could fill.

At sixty-eight years old, Virginia had been alone almost a year, and she felt the weight of her solitary life dragging her slowly toward the earth. Amos had noted recently that her stride, once terminally sixteen, seemed to drastically age, slow and stiffen overnight. She knew her once-full figure had thinned so that the roomy shirts and loose trousers she favored seemed to swallow her.

The girl didn't seem to notice her until she climbed the front steps. "Oh! Hello -- I'm looking for Virginia Emmett."

Virginia rose from her seat, smiling. "You found her."

Setting down her bag and shifting her backpack on her shoulder, the young woman stepped forward with her hand extended. "Hi. I'm Delilah."

Virginia shook Delilah's hand. "Delilah..." she said, prompting for a last name.

"Just Delilah." She slipped her hand from Virginia's and sank it into her pocket.

Virginia paused a moment and then she smiled. "Well, 'just Delilah', what can I do for you?"

Delilah's gaze lightened. "Amos Harrison said you might have a room for rent."

"He said I might?" Her smile broadened.

Delilah laughed. "No, actually he didn't. He said you did. Do. I'd like to rent a room."

"There you go! Straightforward and simple! And if Amos sent you, then you just come on in!"

Virginia opened the door and the instant the girl stepped into the hall, and her eyes widened at the sight of sage colored walls, with ivory trim and rich wood floors covered in throw rugs of gold and peach and cornflower blue, Virginia felt her shoulders relax where she hadn't known they were tense and her breathing slow and deepen. It was as if she found footing she'd thought she'd lost forever, a focus, perhaps, other than herself and her sadness.

On the second floor, Virginia opened the door and stood aside so Delilah could step in. Delilah's breath caught in her throat as she looked around at an impossibly beautiful room of the palest lavender, nearly white in the sun, lilac in the shade, with sheer, light curtains that danced in the faintest breeze near a cherry wood sleigh bed set against a multi-paned window. Outside the window the dogwood flowered, and the maple leaves grew rich and green, blue jays screeching and diving through the branches.

Delilah turned a slow circle. "This is beautiful."

Virginia smiled. "Thank you. I like it. That sleigh bed there is almost as old as I am."

Delilah glanced at the pile of pillows and the lush comforter and suddenly could barely keep her eyes open.

"The bathroom is down the hall," Virginia said, "and when you're settled in I'll show you the kitchen. You've got free rein to do as you please, but you are more than welcome to join me for meals. I'd love the company."

"Thank you." Delilah sneezed, a wet, congested sound.

"Well! That sure doesn't sound good! Why don't you get unpacked and I'll go make you some tea."

"Oh, please don't go to any trouble."

Virginia smiled and touched Delilah's shoulder. "I never do. You just get settled and I'll make tea."

When Virginia returned, Delilah was collapsed on the bed, still fully clothed, a film of sweat beading on her forehead.

Virginia set the tea on the dresser and went to her, laying the back of her hand across Delilah's brow. "Oh, Lord. You are running a helluva fever. That's it. Into bed." She started removing Delilah's shoes.

Delilah pulled herself to sitting. "No, I'm okay. I'm okay."

"Oh shut up. You are definitely not okay. Get those damp clothes off and I'll be right back. And no silliness about me going to any trouble!"

Delilah didn't need much looking after, never had much, but when Virginia returned with towels for her hair and a plush chenille bathrobe in powder blue, Delilah accepted, wrapping herself in deep softness and the scent of lemon fabric softener.

Delilah fell completely to the mercy of Virginia's attentive care as the rain and wind of her arrival settled in her lungs as a bad bout of the flu.

She slept fitfully while Virginia nursed her with salty, homemade chicken soup, chamomile tea, and cold cloths against her sweating brow. She felt the exhaustion heavy in her limbs, the fever keeping her from sound sleep and playing tricks on her brain. Once she woke briefly to find two figures standing beside one another in the doorway, their voices hushed in secret conversation. Disoriented, she didn't recognize them and panicked, kicking the covers, struggling to get out of bed. But the room spun when she got to her feet, someone — she didn't know who — catching her before she fell.

Later she woke from a nap to find Amos sitting on a chair by the dresser. "Amos?" Her head throbbed.

Amos rose and moved to the bed, balancing on the edge. "Yeah."

"What are you doing here? God, I'm such a pain in the ass."

"No you aren't. Virginia loves taking care of people. It's what she does. Who she is. She just ran out to get some things and didn't want to leave you alone. How are you?"

Delilah sighed which in turn triggered a cough, dry and raspy. "Okay." Nausea turned her stomach.

Amos laughed. "Yeah, Virginia said you'd say that. Look, I'm going to call a doctor..."

"No!" Delilah bolted up, ignoring the surge in her head and gut. "No. Please. I don't want to see a doctor."

"Delilah..."

"No doctor." Her eyes closed as she sank back to the pillows. "Promise me." She wanted no more strangers.

She heard Amos sigh. "I promise."

"I'll just sleep. I'll be fine. No trouble." She mumbled. Sleep was moving in fast. A heavy, pervasive weight.

"You do that. Get some sleep."

She peeked through tired eyelids as Amos got up and returned to the chair.

"Promise..." Delilah sighed as she drifted off again. She didn't see Amos just rub his eyes and nod.

On more than one occasion during her illness Delilah woke out of confused nightmares, stumbling out of bed, striking out at odd shadows and trying to muffle the cries rising in her throat. She'd regain clarity and find Virginia's arms around her, guiding her back to bed, staying with her until she fell back asleep. Those same arms guided her to the bathroom when needed, or lifted her, supporting her as she sipped broth and cups of water.

But finally, the fever broke and Delilah looked up for the first time with clear, shining eyes. "Hi." she smiled at the older woman perched on the edge of the bed, watching. Waiting.

Virginia sighed, and smiled, brushing a curl from Delilah's eye as though she were a child. "Hi, yourself. Good to see you come around! I told Amos I'd give you a week and then I was calling a doctor whether you liked it or not. You just made it."

Delilah lifted herself onto one elbow and glanced out the window. "A week? I've been sick a week?"

"Yup. You made us nervous there for a few days." She touched Delilah's hand. "But, well, you're better now, and that's all that matters. However, I want you in bed one more day. Let your body build back some strength."

Delilah lay back down and pressed her hands to her eyes. *A week,* she thought. Rubbing her hands through her hair she glanced at Virginia, her soft gray eyes, thin lips set in a gentle smile. "Thank you."

Virginia leaned in and kissed her on the forehead. "Don't mention it. And welcome to your new home—for as long as you want it to be."

The morning after her recovery, Delilah sat in bed and gazed out the window. Leaves on the trees were young and bright green, sparrows gathered in noisy bunches. She opened the window and breathed in the smell of grass and dew and sun. Her long bus ride of just one week before seemed a far away dream. Awkward, uncertain, she climbed out of bed and crept toward the smell of coffee and the sound of plates being set on a heavy, wooden table, a comforting "thunk" of weight and substance. She paused in the doorway.

Virginia spotted her as she turned to set out coffee cups. "Delilah! Good morning! How are you feeling?"

Delilah broke into a smile she couldn't seem to control. "Better. Pretty good, actually. And hungry."

Virginia clapped her hands together. "*That's* what I like to hear! Sit down—you don't need an invitation, this is your house too, now."

Delilah's knees felt weak, her eyes teared slightly, and she thought perhaps it was what remained of the flu that made her suck in a deep breath and steady herself on the back of a chair.

It was almost too much—this house, this woman, everything perfect and comfortable and right. Again she was afraid to believe it could be this simple. This easy.

She felt a part of her tug to leave, get back on the bus and keep going.

Virginia motioned to the chair and Delilah sat down. Virginia took the chair opposite.

"So, Delilah, what are your plans now?" Virginia paused with her coffee cup an inch from her lips. "Not that you have to have any plans, mind you." She smiled.

"Actually, I need to find some work, I guess. I'm afraid I'm not independently wealthy and will not be able to pay for my room if I don't get a job."

"Well, I'm sure we can take care of that. But don't you worry about it, either. If you need some time to get on your feet, that's okay. This house isn't going anywhere."

"I seem to recall Amos saying he thought the woman who owned the hat store..."

"Millie?"

"Yes, Millie, might need some help."

Virginia finished her coffee and wiped the corners of her mouth with her napkin. "Well, if Amos said it, it's probably true. Would you like to work there?"

Delilah shrugged and pursed her lips. "Why not? I'll do just about anything."

"Then hats it is!" Virginia's smile broadened and her hand came to rest on top of Delilah's.

The girl tensed imperceptibly in response, but smiled nevertheless. "Hats it is."

$\mathcal{D}$elilah was surprised to find how much she enjoyed selling hats, and with Virginia's assistance in cajoling and convincing, Millie agreed to pay Delilah in cash, rather than a pay check.

A simple clerk's job, she found the rhythm of people coming and going, the easy chatter, comforting. She knew people must have questions about her, but they didn't ask, and it seemed her ease with them allayed any concerns they may have had. In fact, she noticed that women seemed to come to her to chat. She noticed a look in their eyes like she reminded them of something -- something gone or misplaced. They made her feel that being around her brought it all back. It was odd, but it made her feel she belonged.

It was as though they had been waiting for her, this town, these people, holding a space at a future bookmark in their lives until the time she arrived.

"Good morning, Amos." Delilah strolled through the door of the store, letting in a momentary blast of pre-summer heat. For several weeks, as June passed full of sunflowers and hyacinths, she'd been coming in every morning for coffee and a corn muffin—toasted with butter—before walking over to Stafford Street. Sometimes she'd brew the coffee for him and straighten the counter: napkins, sugars, creamers all in a row.

Early on Amos talked about Millie's store, how Millie's success had always stymied him since there really wasn't much call for hats anymore (particularly in such a small town). But (as witnessed by Millie's comment that women kept buying her hats) it seemed, at least to Amos, that women could always find an excuse if they wanted something badly enough. Like it was Tuesday, or the sun was shining, or it was so-and-so's dog's birthday.

Delilah said it was that women simply had a natural flair and instinctual appreciation for everyday costuming. She said an ordinary woman could transform herself to the core just by changing (or donning) a hat, that she would carry herself differently, and even her behavior and demeanor would alter.

Amos repeated himself, saying a woman could always find an excuse—no matter how elaborate or contrived—and make it sound perfectly logical. Even one who was only eighteen. If women had a flair for anything, it was that.

Today her white, gauze shirt, sheer and light, and skirt that fell nearly to her ankles almost made her look as though she stepped out of another place and time. She had pinned the sides of her hair up and away from her face, stray wisps framing her eyes.

"Morning, Delilah." Amos slid behind the counter, poured her a cup of coffee and set it on the counter as she took a seat. She noticed his hands, large with long, slender fingers, nearly dwarfed the cup and yet still managed to cradle it gently.

Skeet wouldn't be in for another hour or so, and other townies ate breakfast at home, so they were alone for the moment.

"Before I forget, Virginia asked me to pick up an apple pie on the way home tonight. She doesn't feel like baking, she says, and, 'Amos' pies are the best around next to mine.' Could you keep one aside for her?" She mindlessly aligned sugar bowls, salt shakers, and napkin holders as she spoke.

"Happy to." He wrote a note for himself and left it beside the cash register. There, beside the picture of his wife. Ex-wife? He still didn't know what to call her.

"Thanks." She smiled at him.

"Any time." Before Delilah, Amos happily passed the mornings perched on a stool behind the counter reading, drinking coffee, watching the world go by through the frame of the window. Now he couldn't imagine how he'd ever gotten through a morning without a visit from Delilah. "So, Delilah, coming to the fireworks on the Fourth?" He set a corn muffin down on the counter and took a seat beside her. He knew she came in to visit more than to eat—Virginia made her own, unbeatable muffins—and he enjoyed the fact that mornings were quiet, most of his counter business coming at lunch.

"Hmm... hadn't thought about it. Where do they do it?" In fact, she *had* thought about it—Virginia had already invited her. But she liked the sound of Amos' voice, the way it resonated in some unknown internal depth so she could very nearly sense it in her bones. It made her feel she was floating.

"Over in Carver's park, at the pond. They set up the fireworks beyond the gazebo, near the edge of the woods, and we all sit on the opposite side between the pond and the road. The fireworks themselves are nothing monumental, we are a small operation here, but it's nice. Folks usually set up out there in the afternoon, picnics and whatnot, and then they're there when the show starts."

"Well, maybe I will." Delilah polished off the last of her corn muffin, washing it down with the last of her coffee.

"You oughta. It's a nice day."

"Maybe I will." She smiled easily at him.

Amos noticed how her smile always seemed so at the ready. Almost as though she had trained it to appear on cue. And yet the warmth that accompanied it, the lack of hesitancy and the way she gave herself over to it suggested that it was, indeed, genuine. He tapped the counter and drew a quick, sudden breath.

"Can I get you refill a there?"

"Oh, no thanks, Amos. I gotta get going. Millie is having a 'Festive on the Fourth' sale. Hats aren't just for Easter anymore!"

She swung off the stool at the counter, leaving it spinning on its own, and headed back out into the warm, sunny morning. "See you later for that pie!" she called over her shoulder.

Eighteen and not a care in the world.

What I wouldn't give to be back there again, Amos thought, smiling. *Not enough behind you to matter, and too much ahead to worry about.*

Before heading to work Delilah followed the effusive sounds of summer childhood around the back of the store where a low, chain link fence enclosed an empty, grassy lot used for pick-up games.

A flat, metallic disk of sun blazed behind a thin film of haze, bleaching the pale blue sky.

Five boys had already gathered in the early morning hours to throw the ball around the field. She watched their sneakers kick up dry, sandy dirt as they called to one another, searching the sky for the descending ball.

Beneath a maple tree at the corner of the fence, she closed her eyes and listened to the sounds of their play—taunts and friendly insults, belly laughter and the sudden snap of ball hitting glove. She listened to sneakers scuffing dirt, and grunts as they dove for imitation pop-flies, and cheers made after a major-league catch.

Sounds of childhood.

Sounds so foreign and unreal that the only way she could be certain of them was to open her eyes. The idea of this time called "childhood" was something only heard about second-hand, a story told about a land beyond rainbows. The world may view her as barely out of her childhood, but she, herself, could not recall ever being *in* it, and so it became an oddity, a phenomenon to be studied with the same perplexed curiosity of a scientist studying a black hole.

"Bobby!" The call came from beyond the other side of the fence, a piercing screech that froze all boys mid-play, the airborne ball clunking unnoticed to the ground.

"Get your ass over here right this minute!" A small woman—younger than her stooped shoulders and dark, angry facial lines suggested—staggered forward beneath the weight of a thousand lifetimes crammed into one, dragging a floppy-eared puppy behind her on a leash. The dog leapt and played at her heels, full of innocent abandon, but she ignored it, focused on a small boy in the field who stood motionless. "Either take care of this mutt, or I swear to God I'll leave it in the middle of the highway!"

Delilah's breath caught in her chest as she became riveted, the world dissolving into a tight, focused tunnel that included the woman, the boy, and the dog. The rest wavered, an uncertain mirage in the glare of sun. She knew this person. Not personally, not this particular woman, but the person in general, knew she possessed the power to turn the world black, to leech innocence from the young like a vampire sucks blood.

"I *am* taking care of him, mom." The boy remained where he stood, speaking evenly and carefully, performing the ritual of emotional alchemy, trying to turn the lead of hatred into the gold of love.

"Oh yeah?" The woman stood a few feet away from the fence, her jeans faded, tired eyes sunken in a sallow complexion, and her grip on the leash making Delilah's throat close up. "Then how come he pissed all over the goddamn kitchen floor, you little shit!" Heaving the leash forward, she lodged her toe beneath the puppy's belly and launched it toward the fence where it collided with a yelp and cowered near the ground.

The boy clambered over the fence, retrieved the dog, and returned to the enclosure with speed and agility familiar to Delilah. The dance was never to be forgotten. Her knuckles grew white as she gripped the links in the fence, a heat rising somewhere, burning the inside of her skin, the dust hanging in the air coating her mouth, her throat, and when the woman locked her gaze to Delilah's with eyes so empty and dark and accusing, Delilah's fingers lost their strength, released the fence, and she spun, falling to her knees. Her stomach lurched and she closed her eyes tight, knowing what would follow, waiting for the sour, stinging taste and cold sweat.

By the time Amos glanced out the storeroom window and came out with some water and a cold cloth it was all over and Delilah sat back against the trunk of the maple tree without an explanation.

"Amos?"

"Yeah. It's me. You okay?"

Delilah seemed to struggle to focus, a moment of panic flicking across her face. Then she blinked, swallowed, and, looking at Amos, she shyly shook him off and got to her feet. "How embarrassing. Guess I fainted or something. What'd you put in my coffee, for chrissake?"

"Why don't you come back inside."

"No, I'm fine, really."

Amos shook his head. "Yeah, you're always fine. C'mon."

"I'm fine."

He helped her to her feet and in so doing caught a glimpse of a scar on her right wrist. At least he thought it was a scar, but her hand withdrew from his before he could be sure. It startled him. Made his heart quicken and his mouth go dry. He wanted to grab her arm, to take another look and know for sure, but he knew he couldn't. Shouldn't. And Delilah was already walking away.

Amos was still thinking about it when, at twelve thirty, the lunch crowd began to arrive. In fact, he had been leaning back against the counter, dishtowel hanging from his hands in mid-wipe, gaze unfocused, inward, for nearly three-quarters of an hour.

He was more than usually thankful for the distraction, since the image of Delilah, so frail and insubstantial, had haunted him all morning. He'd seen that frailty once before in his life and he didn't like it then, either. There had also been something eerie in her eyes. She looked at him, but it was as though she saw something else. Even the boys in the sandlot had nothing to offer. They hadn't even noticed she was there. Ephemeral, a will-o-the-wisp, she walked among them unseen. And Harold Reinman, who had been standing a short distance away, one finger playing absently in a curl of his hair, ignored Amos when he called to him. Harold just stared blankly a moment, gritted his teeth and walked away.

But now, the stream of familiar faces helped to draw Amos' attention elsewhere. The store filled with chatter, dishes clanking, laughter, sometimes a disagreement—sounds of life in progress.

It never lasted long, and in a few hours he'd have the rest of the day to bake his pies, tend his store and enjoy the afternoon.

"Afternoon, Amos." Millie slid herself onto a stool and leaned her chin on her hand. She liked the way her attention made him nervous. She meant nothing by it. It was innocent play.

"Millie," he tipped his head at her, "how's your 'Festive on the Fourth' sale?"

Millie laughed. "Booming! I think I got Sinclair coming in now. Goddamn these women love hats! And God bless Delilah, boy. That girl could sell a hat to the headless horseman."

Amos's snorted a short laugh. "Well, I'm glad. For you and for her. Now, what can I get you?"

"Turkey, rye, lettuce, mustard, and a coffee, please."

"Sure thing." He walked away without ever quite looking at her. She was an attractive woman, mid-forties, self-possessed. Her name did not suit her at all. He always felt she would have done well in the world of big-business, but she took over the family store and seemed to like the kind of big-fish-in-a-small-pond attention she drew in Macaenas.

"Amos," she began, as he set her coffee in front of her, "Delilah ever talk to you about herself?"

"Not really." He set out cream and sugar.

"Really? Not even to you?"

"Not even to me, Millie." He knew it was not nearly a satisfactory answer but thankfully, he was able to turn his attention to two police officers who, just moments before, looked at their watches, turned the patrol car into the parking lot and were now walking toward the counter, followed by a woman from the library.

It wasn't that Amos didn't share Millie's curiosity. In fact, be probably had more questions than just about anyone. But Delilah's blatant avoidance of all things personal clearly came from someplace deeper than stubbornness or aloofness, and her underlying timidity made Amos feel protective of her. People as intricate as Delilah did not come with easy answers, and all those layers seemed to make them more fragile.

For now, however, Millie had been rebuffed, and by two o'clock they would all be back to work, he could brew an extra strong pot of coffee, sit at the counter and let his mind drift to thoughts distant and private. The only interruptions then would be kids for sodas and ice cream and people needing a quart of milk or a box of sugar—little eruptions bubbling forth that left comforting echoes behind.

Some days he prayed that during the ebbs of life his mind would remain empty and still. There were times when he preferred empty-headed idleness that allowed him to watch the crimson streaks of darting cardinals, or the slow amble of passing pedestrians, all without unwanted interruption. Just the comforting hum of his internal test pattern.

Later in the afternoon the boys from the lot behind the store tumbled in, full of dirt and sweat and summer thirst, and he gave them a two-for-one deal on sodas and a bowl of water for the dog. The money they saved went to candy which was not what Amos had in mind, but they were kids. Childhood only happened once in your life. He figured they might as well enjoy it while it lasted.

$\mathcal{A}$s a child of ten, Virginia met a girl who had been born blind. As their friendship grew, Virginia became frustrated and sad that this girl had no concept of color; she had never seen a sunset or a rolling expanse of emerald grassland — had no idea of how they looked.

One afternoon as they walked together, they passed Virginia's neighbor as he toiled with a push mower in his yard. Virginia breathed deep the sweet, clean aroma of freshly cut grass and suddenly it hit her. "That's green!" she yelled, grabbing her friend's arm and pulling her to a stop.

"What?"

"Breathe!" Virginia yelled. "Smell that? That's the color green!"

The little girl inhaled, pulling the fragrance deep into her body and she laughed. "Green?" she asked.

"Green!" Virginia shrieked. It was an event that changed both lives forever as Virginia opened the world for a friend -- showing her that pink was the soft fragrance of talcum powder, and snow was the combination of the scent of lilies (white) and mint (blue) -- and learning for herself the power of perception and the inherent magic of the world.

Now, on Stafford Street, in the shadow of an awning and amidst the intoxicating aroma of lilac, Virginia stood outside Millie's store as the sandlot boys and their dog ran by, full of Amos' generosity.

She hadn't intended on that destination, had in fact been going to the library for a book on how to rid her burgeoning tomato plants of garden pests, but instead she'd spent the last fifteen minutes with lips pursed, hands in the pockets of her slightly baggy, beige trousers, staring at the hats in the window. Sometimes she'd shift her focus so she stared at her own reflection, at the deepening lines, the skin sagging slightly, brow furrowed. Then she'd shift focus again so that she saw both, hats and reflection, making it appear one of the hats in the window was on her head, and she'd brush a stray hair from her eye, laughing quietly.

These were the moments when the passage of time most confounded her. Staring at the reflection of her own eyes she saw a girl of eighteen: excited, passionate, full of the life ahead of her. She felt that girl. The one who could smell green. Still thought the same as her, laughed like her, could recall the moments of her life as though they had only happened yesterday.

But then her focus expanded to include the lines at the corners of those eyes, which led to those around her mouth, and the soft folds of skin along her neck, and she nearly could not comprehend that it was the same person. A lifetime had passed, but somewhere within her was a girl stepping out into the world for the very first time.

Delilah stuck her head out the door, "Virginia! It's a helluva lot cooler in here. Why don't you stare at them from inside?"

"Oh please, you just wanna sell me a hat." Virginia waved her away.

"Hm... hadn't actually thought about it, but now that you mention it..." Delilah cocked her eyebrow playfully.

"Oh, Delilah," her gaze flicked to the window again, "I haven't worn a hat in probably forty years."

"Well, then I'd say you're about due, wouldn't you?" She held the door open and waited for Virginia who finally stepped through.

Inside the shop Virginia sat patiently before an antique, gilded mirror as Delilah moved from hat to hat.

"Oh, honey. I've never been much for feathers!" Virginia laughed as Delilah placed a crimson-plumed fedora on her head.

"Why, Virginia Emmett—" Millie stood in the doorway to the back office, "I've *never* seen you in here!"

"Yeah, well, I'm not sure why I'm here now, frankly. I was supposed to be going to the library!"

Virginia glanced at herself again, shifting her head from side to side and finally cocked the fedora down over one eye, sending the plumage to a jaunty angle. "Hey there, big boy...," Virginia cooed, sending the three women into a burst of raucous laughter that caused people on the street to pause and listen to the familiar, mysterious sound of women coming together that other women acknowledged with an easy smile, and men listened to with uncertain curiosity.

No one laughed harder than Virginia, who had to wipe away tears.

After the hat had made its way around to each woman and her personal interpretation, they finally quieted down with full sighs and shaking heads. Then Delilah retrieved a simple, wide-brimmed straw sunhat from a brass hat stand. It had a broad, sand-colored scarf that wrapped around like a hat band and then hung over the brim to tie under the chin. "Very Mary Poppins," she said. "And good for in the garden."

"Oh no... more Kate Hepburn in *African Queen*," Virginia replied, trying to sound indifferent.

Delilah placed it over Virginia's loosely clipped bun and tied a soft, draping bow just off center.

The tip of the brim framed Virginia's pale, grey eyes, and the scarf accentuated the line of her high-set cheekbones. It brought glimpses of a girl long-gone.

Looking at herself Virginia fell speechless.

She saw something in her reflection—something she hadn't seen in a while: herself. She'd been alone for just long enough to pull away from the world, but suddenly a spark had returned, however faintly, flickering in the pale, gold flecks in her eyes.

"Well, Delilah," Millie folded her arms and leaned against the door frame, "I've said it before, and I'll say it again, you've got a helluva knack for picking out the perfect hat."

The afternoon drew long, thin shadows across the ground—distorted, elongated silhouettes of familiar objects—and an easy, early-summer breeze tickled eaves and wisps of hair, strew long, vaporous ribbons of clouds across a sheer blue sky. Dogs lazed beneath shady limbs, Sergeant Tilton leaned against the hood of his police car in the station parking lot drinking a Coke out of a bottle dripping with condensation, and an older woman in a new straw hat strolled lazily along the library walkway, her step so light she nearly appeared to hover a fraction of an inch above the ground.

Once inside the library, Virginia loosened the hat and let it hang against her back. Her giddiness from the hat shop still lingered, making her light-headed as though she'd had too much wine.

On her way toward the gardening section she spotted Harold Reinman in the middle of an aisle hunched over a book. As long as she'd known him, her sorrow over his fate never abated. He had been a bright, inquisitive child until the culmination of abuse when he was fifteen. Now he was a child-man. Lost. Sad. Distant.

"Hello, Harold," she whispered as she approached.

Although Harold had noticed her coming softly toward him he only glanced at her out of the corner of his eye. He liked Virginia a great deal, liked her powdery smell and her gentle touch. He didn't dare like her too much, however. That idea scared him, although he couldn't quite explain why. He didn't know the complexities of his psyche, the clinical explanations for his fears; he didn't know, really, the power of buried memories and emotional scars. He only knew the world confused him.

"I just wanted to tell you," Virginia continued, careful not to get too close, "I'm planning to do a little baking this weekend. Chocolate chip cookies. If you feel like stopping by Saturday afternoon you might catch them while they're still warm."

Harold rocked silently from heel to toe. He like Virginia's house as much as he liked Virginia. The way it always smelled sweet and all the colors were warm. He never felt afraid at Virginia's.

"Well," Virginia took a step away, "I just wanted to let you know. You just come by if you want." She smiled and turned back the way she came, disappearing around the next stack of books.

Harold looked up to where she had just stood, "Okay," he said, and returned to the book held open in his hands.

Amos nearly didn't recognize Delilah when she returned early that evening for the apple pie. He'd just finished counting the register and locking up the receipts. It had been the kind of day that gnawed at him, tugging at what remained of the child inside, pressing him to close up early and lay in his backyard hammock with a cold beer resting on his stomach, to play hooky, play ball, just play. He hadn't done so, however, and was now anxious to leave.

"Can I help you?" He'd only glanced quickly at her.

"I believe you have an apple pie for me, Mr. Harrison?" She stood at the counter, right hand on right hip, which she slung out an angle that drew attention to her tiny waist.

Her hair was up and hidden beneath a peach-colored straw hat, the brim so wide it dipped over her eyes, shadowing them, a small gathering of dried, pink roses holding a mesh sash in place around the bowl of the hat.

"Delilah? Can't be!" Amos set the pie on the table and took a few steps back. As though distance would convince him of her identity.

"I told you about hats, Amos. They are magical, causing complete, although temporary, transformations." She retrieved the pie from the counter and handed Amos exact change. "Much like masks, now that I think of it."

Who the hell do you think you are? The voice, so clear, so familiar yet somewhat distant, cut through Delilah's heart and she faltered, her smile mown down before fully completed, and she kept her eyes lowered. She hadn't heard that voice in what seemed like a lifetime, and the fear sprang forward as if it had never left. Had she actually heard it? Had time and distance collapsed like the house of cards they were?

"What?" She whispered.

"I said, yeah, I suppose you're right." Amos hadn't noticed the subtle, sudden shift in her manner.

Delilah blinked, looking up at Amos as though only just realizing he was there, and her smile returned as though it had never left. But inside -- inside the fear raged and she fought a battle no one else could see.

Outside the window, Harold, in a plain blue t-shirt and faded jeans, paused to glance inside, his gaze by turns inquisitive, distant, empty. Then he continued on his way.

"See ya tomorrow, Mr. Harrison," Delilah sang, a forced trill of laughter spilling in her wake as she headed out the door. "And remember, it's all an illusion!"

Amos watched her leave, her gait a bit lankier, her stride a mite lazier, her entire physique seemingly made of dripping honey.

"I'll be damned," he muttered to himself as he put the cash in the register, "that's one helluva hat."

Even at four years old Delilah knew enough to be afraid.

Like most adults in regard to children, Delilah's parents underestimated her capacity for insight and understanding, or perhaps simply didn't care, or didn't think of it. So when the fighting began it never occurred to them that she might have not only heard, but listened and struggled to comprehend.

When the night-sounds from downstairs grew pitched and shrill, Delilah imagined her mother fighting off some terrible monster. She envisioned some sort of demon-ogre like those of fairytales, and she wished she had the courage and the strength to stand by her mother's side in fending off the beast.

She wondered why her father never came to help. Where was he when this night-crawler attacked? But she never dared venture out to see. Better to pull the covers tight and pray the monster didn't realize she was there. She knew it was cowardly, even then, but she didn't know what else to do.

It was not until a year later, after her fifth birthday party, that she made the terrible connection between the beast and her father. It wasn't until the beast had finished leaving bruises on her mother and stomped up the stairs, footfalls thundering down the hallway, growing louder as they approached her room, the door swinging open, the hall light casting a huge shadow of him over her bed where she lay cowering, wishing herself smaller, wishing herself away, wishing; it wasn't until the beast grabbed a fistful of her hair to drag her from bed and large, rough knuckles drew the metallic taste of blood from her five-year-old lip; it wasn't until then, from her spot on the floor where she'd landed, that she looked up as the beast shifted his stance, the hall light falling on his face –- only then did she see the reason her father had never come to rescue her mother from the night-ogre.

Only then did she know.

On the way home Delilah stopped at the newsstand and picked up a vapid fashion rag—a guilty pleasure in which she rarely indulged, but that helped distract her when the ghosts felt too strong.

"Well don't you look stunning," Charlie Horn commented as he handed back her change. His grey hair still came in thick and full, small waves skimming up over his ears. He wore a shortsleeve shirt of pale yellow, a cigar poking out of the top of his breast pocket.

"Why thank you very much, Mr. Horn." She played. "I sold a similar one to your wife today. More lavender, though."

"Really? Does it make her look as good as you?"

"Better! I bet it makes her look as beautiful as the day you married her."

Charlie slapped the counter. "Damn! It's a time machine hat!"

Delilah laughed. "Oh, you be nice. Go home and tell her she's beautiful."

"Oh. Yes, ma'am. Of course—I do that anyway. I tell her she still looks like a young Elizabeth Taylor."

Delilah paused. "Really?"

"Every day."

"Well. Good." Delilah took the magazine and turned to leave. "Night, Charlie."

"Night, Delilah," he called. "Take care."

After dinner Delilah took her pie and fashion magazine and climbed the creaky stairs to her room.

As a rule, she avoided mirrors, put off by the sight of herself, by the way the eyes of the reflection never seemed to be her own.

As a child she had once walked into a dimly lit room and, seeing movement out of the corner of her eye, she spun around, catching her reflection in a mirror—her eyes registering before the rest of her—and it had terrified her: huge, dark orbs that seemed to want to sink back into her skull.

But now she set the pie and the magazine on the edge of her bureau and took a tentative step in front of the full length, brass-framed mirror. She tried to view herself from outside herself, to see what others saw, tipping her head left and right like a dog hearing a high-pitched sound. The image she saw did not unsettle her as much as it once had.

The mirror reflected the sleigh bed and an oak rocking chair with tapestry cushions behind her, things strong and comforting that seemed to buoy her. Solidify her. Reaching out to touch her reflected image, she nearly expected—just for a moment—to feel the warm pulse of flesh rather than the cool smoothness of glass. Like Alice she might have stepped through to another world.

But she didn't.

Flipping through the magazine she stopped at a page full of a long, thin model, soft ringlets of hair piled haphazardly on her head, stray strands cascading delicately around her face.

Delilah returned to her reflection, gathering her hair in a mass of curls, bunching it atop her head in a fair representation of the photo and studying the result: a young woman, certain, perhaps a bit shadowed and more woman than girl. That surprised her. She didn't recall the girl having left. Had it happened gradually? Or all at once? Where had she gone?

DELILAH!

It crashed through her skull and she stumbled backwards as though struck, knocking the pie from the bureau to the fringed rug, sauce smearing across the woven roses. Her hands shook as the stared at the spill. Her throat tightened, making it difficult to swallow or take a breath, as though a hand had closed around her neck.

She could no longer focus on the image of her reflection—it wavered, obstructed by an amorphous darkness that slid around the edges of the glass and threatened to bleed out into the far corners of the room, obliterating the magazine, her, the rocker, the sleigh bed, all of the tenuous reality around her. It was a voice comprised of evil and evoking a primal, paralyzing fear that clenched her jaw, tensed every sinew in her body in an instinctual readiness to flee.

She heard footsteps in the hall. The booming at the door. She flinched. The door clicked slowly open and Delilah saw looming shadows roiling like summoned demons. Her stomach lurched, and she prayed for her knees to buckle so she could curl around on herself, make herself smaller... smaller...

Virginia decided to have some tea and thought Delilah might like to join her. As she climbed the stair she heard a sound from Delilah's room –- a kind of thud and small crash.

She knocked softly on the door, but when there was no answer she gently clicked the door open and peered into the room. "Honey? You okay? I was going to offer you some tea and then I heard—Delilah?"

What she saw stopped her. Delilah's whole body shook—one, large tremble. Her eyes, trained on the door, stood wide, vacant and unseeing. Like the possessed, the entranced of lore and legend, she appeared overtaken by a force large and full of darkness.

"Delilah? Hey..." Virginia stepped into the room and enfolded Delilah in her arms. "You look like you've seen a ghost!"

Inside the warm softness of Virginia's embrace full of the scent of talcum powder and lavender oil, the spell left Delilah, gone like the nervous flitting of a hummingbird. She glanced to the carpet then to Virginia, looking as though she was waking from a dream.

"What a klutz." Sliding artfully from Virginia's arms, she began to clean up the mess, struggling to steady the whirl in her mind.

"Delilah, are you all right?" Virginia felt an instinct to draw her close, to draw the truth from her, knowing there were complexities of which she was unaware, but Delilah set clear boundaries.

"Oh, yeah. Just off daydreaming again. Not paying attention. I'll get it all clean though." She grabbed a handful of tissues from the nightstand and swabbed at the spill.

Virginia knelt beside her. "I'm not worried about the mess. I am a little worried about you, however."

Delilah's jaw clenched a moment, a brief gesture of impatience, then she smiled, leaning in to leave a kiss on Virginia's cheek. "Don't. I just wander away sometimes. Always have. I have a terrific imagination that sometimes gets the better of me. That's all. Now—what did you say about tea?"

"Delilah..." Virginia caught the girl's wrist as she moved to clean the spill and felt Delilah freeze at the touch. It was then Virginia noticed the scars -- two of them, one on each wrist starting at the heel of Delilah's hand and traveling two inches down her wrist. It made her catch her breath and she released her grip, allowing Delilah withdraw. An ache spread across Virginia's heart that left her cold inside. "I have never pressed you on anything. Ever. I've respected your privacy in every way. But you spooked me just now. Don't tell me that was nothing." The scars frightened her—spoke more, revealed more than any story Delilah could tell.

Delilah began to tremble again, Virginia's voice too kind, too full of love.

"Oh, sweetheart," Virginia continued, "you can tell me anything. Don't you know that yet?"

"I..." Delilah began, feeling as though she was learning the words for the very first time. "It's..." She wanted to, wanted to let the images come clear, to remember all she'd forgotten or denied. She wanted to say it, get it out, rid herself of it, even just a little bit.

"Go on, honey."

But the words failed her. "I can't."

"Delilah..."

"No!" She pulled away and rose to her feet. "Don't ask me! I can't!"

Leaving the remains of the pie and the plate she turned and left the room.

In the strained, uncertain silence that followed, Virginia jumped when the magazine suddenly shifted, pages fluttering shut. She clutched her throat. "Good Lord, what next?" There were, of course, a wealth of possibilities for what might happen next, a multitude of paths that could unfold, but never knowing the future for certain, Virginia knew, as her mother had always told her, they all forever walked blindly forward with nothing but a tentative faith that the next step will find familiar and solid ground.

And so, laughing at herself, stifling confused tears, she gave the magazine a tap on the cover and went down to find Delilah.

She could not find her, though. She found, instead, an empty house with an open front door, Delilah gone out into the night alone, walking, wandering, pushing down ghosts that struggled to the surface, fighting with a past she'd rather leave behind.

Whatever lived inside that girl wasn't coming out just for the asking. But every day of silence made Virginia fear for Delilah a little more.

$\mathcal{E}$arly Saturday morning Delilah left Virginia's and found a young man about to open the gate as she approached. He was wiry and angular, a pipe-cleaner-man with mopish hair that flipped haphazardly in the breeze. He stopped short when he saw her, one hand going to his hair, twirling in the curl above his ear. He did not look at her.

"Hi," Delilah said, opening the gate and stepping aside to let him through first. "Go ahead."

The young man didn't seem to know what to do. He pursed his lips. He squeezed his right side as though he suddenly developed a pain there. He twirled his fingers through his hair. Then, rocking twice from foot to foot as if he were building momentum, he finally took a deep breath and pushed himself past her toward the porch.

Delilah stood a moment, then walked out the gate. Turning, she watched him walk right into the house, no knocking, no pretense, just walked right in, turning to peek quickly at her as he shut the door behind him.

"Bye," she said to the empty porch, vaguely aware of tugging somewhere deep inside her that said he was someone familiar.

Leaving Virginia's, Delilah traveled down Haven Lane with its country curves and deep shade, the scent of lilac assaulting her in sweet, intoxicating waves. The long, unplanned, unaccounted-for days of the weekend left her somewhat stranded: still something of a stranger in town, uncertain if she cared to be anything more, but full of a desire to ingest this picket-fenced, window-shuttered, flower-boxed town so that it became a part of her. She struggled with the strange duality of a fierce privateness and a yearning to feel connected—two things forever at odds within her, splitting her down the center almost like two distinct people. It was a tension that often sent her spinning like a top, momentum that propelled her into long, solitary walks as though answers might lie along the edges of woods or in gutter drains. Whole afternoons would be lost to her wanderings, her mind turned so far inward that were someone to ask her where she'd been, she could only blink, smile blankly, and say, "I don't really remember," a habit which kept people at arm's length whether that was her intention or not.

When this behavior began she couldn't recall, there was no definitive moment in her memory when this dichotomy formed, she only knew it had. And like a character in someone else's story, she found she could only look at the world around her as an almost impassive observer, one with an occasional longing to step forward and find her own place in the tale.

Millie knelt in her front yard to weed around bushes full of snowball-like flowers. Her monstrous tabby, Rufus, chased the trailing roots as she pulled them free with a spray of dirt. Turning to toss a handful of gnarled greens into a basket, she caught a glimpse of Delilah paused in thought across the street. She spied quietly a moment, trying to glean the girl's inner core through sheer force of will; she tried to remember what it was like to be eighteen years old and was crushed to discover she could no longer recall. Too long ago now. Gone in the fading distance. "Delilah! Hello!" she finally called. "How are you this afternoon?" Millie had tried unsuccessfully over the past few weeks to engage Delilah in revealing conversation, to draw out insights about her, for although it seemed she had, obviously the girl did not simply fall from the sky. But Delilah was an expert evader, and Millie had never caught her outside of work.

Delilah looked up from her hand where she'd been harboring a ladybug crawling on her fingers which now leapt from her pinky and vanished. "Hi, Millie. I'm good, thanks. It's a good day."

"Hm. Yes. Why don't you come visit with me?" She motioned to a wooden bench-swing hung by two enormous ropes from a heavy branch of a maple tree. Delilah hesitated, never wanting to bruise feelings, always acutely aware of how easily it could happen and never certain of the sincerity of Millie's seemingly innocent intentions. Millie had a tendency toward inquisitiveness, needed to be in the know in every situation, but Delilah did not care to be in the spotlight, was not a situation that desired to be known. "It's okay honey, I don't bite. Regardless of what you may have heard," Millie continued, smiling.

"Oh, I know that." Delilah gave a small laugh. "I think I'm just in the mood for a walk." A life built on motion and solitude did not easily relax to stillness and company. Even had she wanted to, Delilah would find it difficult to open certain doors within herself, so as a rule she simply learned not to want to. It was a surprisingly easy thing to teach herself, and something that often took on a life of its own.

Millie waved her away with a quiet snort, "You and Amos with your 'walks.' I don't get it! Conserve energy, drive a car! That's my motto!" She laughed at herself and tossed a weed off into the yard for Rufus to chase down. The cat scrambled from beneath the bushes, a bouncing ball of tortoise shell fur, leapt over the walkway to pounce on the motionless weed and then rolled lazily over onto his back in the shade, his job as hunter completed.

"You know," Millie continued as she returned to her weeding, "I do not profess to be any kind of gardener. These shrubs were my mother's doing, but I feel a certain responsibility to at least attempt their upkeep. My folks are spending their golden years in the sun and hurricanes of the south and invariably ask of the shrubs whenever they call. It's unnerving. In fact, I'm starting to think that the bushes' survival and my parents' are supernaturally intertwined. I'm afraid if the shrubs ever died, they wouldn't be far behind."

Delilah smiled to herself and continued on her way without another word to Millie, who continued with her gardening as though Delilah had never been there. To have people seamlessly resume their lives after a brief interaction with her was not uncommon for Delilah, and it often made her wonder if the prior conversation had happened at all. It made her wonder if she were any more substantial than a quick gust of wind.

Now as she walked, Delilah's thoughts drifted to the bus ride into Macaenas. Days of endless rain running webbed tracks along the windshield, the soft, mesmerizing rocking as they whisked along the highway, the world outside the window disappearing as night moved in making everything varying densities of blackness. The rest stops full of tired, aggravated travelers, children with tear streaks washed along dirty cheeks, faces puffed in over-tired pouts. She wondered of the other passengers – the young couple with pierced eyebrows and lips, sharing the earphones of a walkman, girl with the left ear, boy with the right—did they each hear only half the music? Or the man in the wrinkled suit, shirttail stained and hanging out, his lips constantly moving with silent utterances. And how had she appeared to them as she slept on her lumpy backpack, curled over two seats? A young girl alone probably visiting friends or relatives, or perhaps returning from school? Or did she appear as she felt: tired, frightened and alone? They all had a story; each a world unto themselves revolving and evolving within the spin of this larger, shared orb. Worlds within a world. No one was ever just what you saw when you looked at them. No one.

As glad as she had been to step onto solid ground, to cease the constant, incessant movement, sometimes she longed to be back on that bus, hurtling through blind nights, not thinking of where she was, where she was headed, every passenger a part of the same journey, but each one alone in his solitude. Sometimes she just wanted motion. To pass through life untouched. Sometimes.

"Hey! Could you toss us the ball?"

She blinked into the present, standing on the corner of Main and Haven Lane across from Carver's Park, not realizing the boy and girl standing on the other side had called to her three times. "I'm sorry?"

"Are you deaf? Christ! The ball—can you throw it over here?" The boy rolled his eyes impatiently as he pointed to the curb at her feet where the baseball had landed.

"Oh. Sure." She bent down and plucked the ball from the street, tossing it back with a tenuous smile.

The boy caught it and without a word—just a small, conspiratorial giggle—turned with the girl and ran back into the park. It shouldn't matter, their attitude, their callousness, they were just children. But Delilah stood fighting for breath as though she'd been kicked in the stomach. What is the point of their cruelty? Their mockery? Where is it written that as one ages one must lose the simple kindness of childhood? Is it simply to be chalked up to wild-natured youth or is it behavior learned by example, by watching the ways of the world and the adults who pave the way before them? Even here. In this quiet town. They learn. Somewhere deep behind her right eye a nerve twisted and pinched, became a sharp pain in the middle of her skull.

Out of the corner of her eye she caught a glimpse of someone standing at the edge of the road, looking at her. When she turned to face him—seeing him first not with her eyes but with something more visceral and full of clarity, feeling the intensity of his stare—she felt she knew him in a way that sent a cold wind through her. Knew that look. Then she realized she knew who it was. It was the same young man she met outside Virginia's almost a half hour ago. The one who wouldn't look at her save for a sly, quick glance through the crack of the closing door. But he looked straight at her now.

"Hello, Delilah." Suddenly Amos stood beside her.

"Oh – hi, Amos. Who is that?"

Amos followed Delilah's gaze to where Harold stood. "Oh. That's—that's Harold Reinman."

As though he heard, at the mention of his name, Harold abruptly came to life and disappeared into the woods leaving a strange vacuum behind and a hollow longing inside Delilah. The ache in her head lessened, leaving the odd, untethered thought that perhaps she was losing her mind.

She took a deep breath, casually wiping away silent tears and wrinkled her nose. A heavy, pungent sweetness suddenly filled the air. "Yuck. Skunk."

Amos laughed. "Yup. Probably Rufus spooked one, that crazy feline. That smell will hang in the air all day.

Especially in this heat. Makes the air like a goddamn sponge. I swear, you'd think the population of skunks would have to die out sooner or later, but it seems like I smell them a couple of times a week."

"You should put that in your town brochure— 'Come to Macaenas, the Skunk Capital of the Northeast! You can smell skunks three or four times a week!'" They shared a laugh as Delilah pulled a rubber band from her jeans pocket and pulled her red curls into a cascading pony tail. The heaviness of moments before suddenly vanished and she flashed on a saying she'd read somewhere: *Slipping into madness is good for the sake of comparison.* "Where are you off to today?"

"Just the post office. Errands. You?"

"Nowhere." She smiled, liking the sound of that.

"Well, there's a lot of that around here."

They turned the corner together and walked down Main Street, Delilah turning only once to glance back to where Harold had stood as though some remnant of him might remain from which she could discover more than what she was willing to ask.

She and Amos walked in silence, comfortable with one another, each appreciating the quiet company the other provided until they reached the post office, where Amos stopped at the edge of the flagstone walkway. Sometimes all that was needed was the knowledge of another's presence. "This is my stop." He smiled and pulled several letters out of his back pocket.

"So it is. And I'm off to—wherever. Have a great day, Amos." Delilah beamed and crossed the street toward Stafford.

"You too, Delilah. You too." He watched as she walked away, curls deflecting copper glints of sun, hands slipped in the pockets of her khaki shorts, no different from any other young woman he'd ever seen. Yet he remained forever curious about her, feeling he should always say more, do more, offer more—feeling she expected more, wanting more himself, never knowing what.

Delilah walked up Stafford Street behind the library back wall, which was nearly invisible behind a stand of poplar and pines, a glade full of cool, deep shadows. She walked to Ellington Street to the white clapboard church, its bell tower a silhouette against a glaring sun, stained-glass windows flashing hints of rich, somber colors, and found herself turning left—toward the cemetery and the farm country beyond.

There was no sidewalk on this side of Ellington, just soft shoulder and a worn path in the grass at the side of the road. Traffic was light, an occasional pick-up truck (often smelling of hay or manure) or kids on their bikes racing toward Sinclair the only transient passersby.

The day reflected brightly, the sky pale with heat, its intensity fading the blue to a sun-streaked whitewash. A breeze bent the heads of lanky wildflowers, purple and yellow and white in the surrounding fields, rippling through the grass on the hills, creating a scene so picturesque she questioned its reality.

A thin haze of scallop-edged clouds layered itself near the horizon like a sheet of cotton batting. She stared at them, wondering how she knew that batting was used to line quilts. Somewhere in her memory she had an image of her mother, a long braid falling over her shoulder as she hunched over piles of fabric squares, matching them together into larger pieces, rolls of white stuffing on the floor nearby.

But the image did not come clearly, leaving Delilah uncertain if it was an actual memory, or just an image of something she'd heard once, a picture she'd seen, something she'd dreamed.

Crows and catbirds called and screeched at one another across the road. Breezes rustled leaves like stiff taffeta skirts and she paused a moment by the stone wall of the cemetery, listening, all these sounds winding together in a kind of audible silence that made Delilah hold her breath and wonder, just for a moment, where she was.

"Afternoon, Amos." Ed Carrolton stood behind the counter at the post office, a small line of perspiration running along his receding hairline, his pale blue uniform shirt hanging off his thin, wispy body as if on a hanger in the closet.

"How are you, Ed?" Amos dropped the letters on the counter.

"Can't complain. Nearly finished re-doing the back porch. Finally! You'll have to come over one evening and have a beer." He took out stamps for each envelope, wildflowers this month, wet each one in turn on a small yellow sponge and stuck them to the letters.

Amos smiled. "Hmm. No man should be without a porch for summer evenings. It's one of life's little-known necessities. And I'd say you finished it just in time! Now you've got it for the whole season!" Amos smiled. It was little more than friendly banter -- he could almost hear the shallow ringing of his words like a sour note on a child's toy piano. He would never go to Ed's house, sit on his porch and share a beer. That's just how it was. And although Amos enjoyed the conversation, the simple familiarity, it often made him sad that it would not move beyond that. At least not for him.

Ed dropped the letters in the outgoing bin and smiled at Amos. "Yup. That's why I busted my ass to finish it! Anything else today?"

"Nope." Amos plunked down his money. "That's it for today. Thanks."

Retrieving his change, he turned and walked back out into the harsh, flat sunlight thinking he really *should* drop in on Ed one day. Surprise him. But he wouldn't. It would throw the world off its axis if he started flouting the basic laws of passing conversation. It was funny because he truly did enjoy interaction with others, enjoyed the way it made the world smaller to know peoples' names and how many kids they had and what their plans were. Yet, once he felt the world shrink down, once he felt the calm of that familiarity and re-established his solidity, he quickly felt nervous, stifled, and wanted to step away from it into his own, private corner. It hadn't always been like that, his separateness.

As Amos meandered home, he wondered if *anyone* Ed spoke to ever went over in the evenings. Did they sit on his porch, feet up on the railings, cold beer dripping condensation onto the wooden table as they smoked cigarettes and stubby cigars, swatted away mosquitoes and talked about—what? That was where Amos always came up short. Pausing to look another person square in the eye in search of a commonality from which to converse, he always found himself speechless—full of things to say, but nothing that seemed like it would make a connection. Instead, he would fall uncomfortably silent or, as he did all the time now, he'd avoid social occasions altogether.

It had been easier once. And he suddenly realized why. Once he'd had a kind of bridge between himself and the world, a tether that prevented him from spinning off into solitary space. But she was gone now, his Ellen, and the world was harder to reach without her.

Delilah found herself wandering through the older part of the cemetery, gazing at gravestones as old as the town.

Too many of those graves held the tiny remains of children, one only nine days old. Lifetimes upon lifetimes in crowded rows marked by stones weathered and moss-covered with time, tilting in soil that had shifted over nearly one-hundred years, making them look as tired and defeated as the bones they guarded. Rows of old, crooked teeth. One set of gravestones marked the site of mother and daughter, both dying in childbirth, (*Beloved mother and child...*) and it was those stones that stopped her, (*lost to death in birth...*) forcing her to kneel in the plush, manicured grass to run her fingers over the worn down carvings of their names: Elizabeth and Ruth (*forever embraced in the eternal...*). In her touch, she became full of them, their lives and hearts, her body growing tight, her skin suddenly too snug, her lungs begging for more air than she could give them. She saw the husband/father standing beneath a black umbrella in a charcoal suit, white shirt-collar buttoned high, as a dense, grey sky rained down upon the funeral, and he said goodbye to the two most important things in his world, his wife and his daughter. This husband/father cried. Tears of hollowness.

"Delilah!" Virginia stepped off the path on her way to visit Carl's grave—something she found herself doing more of as time passed, rather than less. "What are you doing here?"

A moment of silence passed in which something intangible fell across Delilah's face. She seemed to transform, to regress to an age much younger and a girl more frail, quiet, nothing more than a wisp. "Thinking of my mother."

Virginia held her breath, the air heavy with expectancy, the moment so fragile that she feared the slightest movement would damage it.

Delilah traced the letters on the headstone with her finger, her voice barely audible so that Virginia had to strain to hear. "My mother's name was Elizabeth. When I was nine years old she took me by the hand and said she had an important lesson to share with me about life. I remember being nervous about leaving the house because..." She paused as though she'd forgotten, or lost the thought, but with a deep breath she continued, "... because my father didn't like to come home to an empty house. But mama said it was important. That I needed to know. So I followed her out back, down the hill full of buttercups and daisies, down to the river that ran below.

"She sat me on a rock near the edge and held my face in her hands, her eyes so full of tears that she scared me. 'I love you, baby. I love you.' She said it over and over.

"Then she kissed me on the forehead and walked into the river, pushing down her skirt as it billowed up around her. I thought her skirt floating around her made her look like the ballerina that twirled in my jewelry box.

"She walked until she couldn't touch, then she swam, never looking back, diving down beneath the surface. I remember thinking..." tears broke free then. The first she'd ever shed for her mother. They began small, gentle trails skimming her cheek, but with each breath, each word spoken, each truth told, they grew more intense. "I was thinking—there must be a cave down beneath the surface because she was under for so long."

Virginia moved toward her then, no longer fearful of breaking a spell, only feeling Delilah's gaping need, encircling her in an embrace before she flew apart into a million shattered pieces.

"Then I thought," Delilah began again, her voice slurred by phlegm and remembrance, "she must have decided to stay in that cave because over an hour later she hadn't come back, and daddy was home, and..." But there was no more. Just sobs and jagged breaths that drowned the words, spilling over and out after nearly ten years in hiding, squeezing Delilah, making her smaller, smaller, threatening to snuff her out like a flame in a tempest.

Virginia cradled Delilah in her arms, her own heart full of shock and pain and grief. She, too, could find no words.

There were none to say.

Heading back toward his house, Amos spotted Harold sitting on the bench outside his store. Books piled beside him, chocolate chip cookie in hand, hair in need of a trim, Harold drew tiny circles in the dirt with the toe of his sneaker.

Amos walked over to the bench and sat beside him, the books a barrier between them. "Hey, Harold. You know I'm closed today, don't you?"

Harold remained silent, just rocked back and forth a few times.

"I was thinking of stopping by your place tomorrow," Amos continued, "see how you were doing. You need anything?"

Again Harold failed to reply, but his rocking ceased, he took a breath and glanced up at Amos with eyes that seemed to see right through him. "Delilah?"

Amos blinked. "Delilah? What about her?" he asked, failing to make the connection to the question he'd just put to Harold.

Harold was not much for conversation, a twenty-five year old whose mind had been reduced to a child's, and he rarely connected with the world beyond the tip of his sneakers, so Amos was fairly surprised to find he even knew about Delilah.

But Harold simply smiled, his eyes focusing for just an instant on Amos', then he gathered his books and meandered off down the road toward home.

"See ya, Harold," Amos said, as if to no one in particular because even if Harold had heard, he wouldn't have cared.

The following afternoon, Amos, like everyone else in town, closed shop early to go home and prepare a feast for the Fourth. He also used the time to pack a few bags of groceries and take them over to Harold's.

For nearly six years -- since he was seventeen -- Harold had lived alone at the end of a dirt driveway that cut its way through the dense woods off Main Street just before it turned into Route One. Nestled in a small clearing of patchy, yellow grass and brown pine needles, the old, grey house sat silently, tilted slightly as if reclining, its porch steps hanging together, it seemed, by only one or two nails. Chips of yellow paint on the trim hinted of a previous life—one brighter and more colorful.

Amos always noticed other hints, too: old marbles long-since abandoned beneath the front steps and a red tricycle lying on its side in the dirt, the axle rusted through, both hinting at childhoods long left behind. Or lost. Forgotten.

Ages fifteen and sixteen of Harold's life were spent in a hospital, cold and white and stark, including six months in a coma. Before that — before that, the world knew a different Harold that he, himself, could no longer recall.

He had since become the town recluse, the pity case, the one, sad story every town seemed to have, the one who wandered the streets eliciting sad glances and shaking heads from those who knew the history, while people like Amos and Virginia took it upon themselves to look after him. To try and help him heal.

Amos turned down the drive and called toward the clearing, "Harold?"

The woods remained silent as Amos reached the porch where he paused and turned around. "Harold?" he called again.

Harold heard but sat silently nearby, in an old deer stand built in an oak tree. He sat cross-legged on the floor, several books strewn around him. One book lay open on his lap, his finger moving swiftly down the page, guiding his eyes, his lips soundlessly mouthing as his body rocked back and forth. "'Alone, alone, all, all alone; Alone on a wide, wide sea.' Samuel Taylor Coleridge. *The Rime of the Ancient Mariner*. He whispered quietly to no one, flipping pages and rocking. Rocking. *Delilah*, he thought. And he smiled.

"Harold, are you home?" Amos tried again, and this time Harold impatiently slammed the book shut and descended from the stand.

Harold walked past Amos and sat on the top step of the slanted porch. He never spoke, never even acknowledged Amos, only sat there, drumming his fingers on his knee.

"Hey there." Amos set down the bag and sat beside Harold. "I don't know if you need it but I brought you some peanut butter because I know you like it."

Harold never looked up at Amos, just tapped his foot on the steps and smiled at his hands.

"Well, I'll bring this stuff inside, okay?" Amos rose and took the bag inside the house, and only after his back was to him did Harold turn and watch him go inside.

A few moments later, Amos returned. "Okay, Harold. You're all set."

Harold's gaze returned to his hands.

Amos laid his hand briefly on Harold's shoulder. "I'll check on you next week sometime, okay?"

Harold looked up quickly to Amos, meeting his gaze for just a second, all the acknowledgement he could muster.

Delilah had just come out of the farmer's market as Amos walked past. "Hey, Amos. Where are you coming from?" She looked beyond him down the road.

"Oh — I just brought Harold some things. Checked in on him. What are you up to?"

She held up a bag, "Buying fruit!" She smiled, glancing again over Amos' shoulder to the woods down the road. Harold's house.

Amos rubbed a sore spot on his shoulder. "Well, I'm going home to make up some snacks for the festivities tomorrow. I'll see you there, right?

Distracted, Delilah blinked back to the conversation. "Oh, yeah. See you there."

"Good." Amos patted her on the shoulder and continued home.

Delilah was already walking in the direction Amos had come from before the conversation was finished. The decision came quickly, seemingly with little initiative from her, and before long she came upon the driveway into the woods.

She stood at the edge of the road, peering toward the clearing, the faded boards of the porch just visible at the end of the drive.

She moved slowly down the driveway, each step amplifying her heartbeat pounding in her ears. Why was she here? What did she need to say? To hear? To know? No answers came, but her body kept moving forward anyway, closer, just to the edge of the clearing, until -- the front door clicked open.

Delilah panicked, dashed into the woods at the side of the drive, as Harold stepped out onto the front porch. She crouched beside a pine, feeling foolish, afraid, but full of a need to know more about this man.

Harold paced back and forth across the porch, his mouth moving as he talked quietly to himself. She watched as he paced, hand twirling in his hair, lips moving, always moving. Talking.

Delilah closed her eyes a moment. What had happened to him? Or did she already know? In her heart, didn't she already know?

She opened her eyes again to see his gaze flick quickly in her direction, pausing as though he'd seen her, but then he turned away and sat in a rocker near the front door.

She watched him. Rocking. Talking. Twirling. She watched him until she couldn't any longer, until it hurt to see, until it ached in her stomach.

They were the same, this oddity and her. They were the same.

July Fourth arrived lightly, the sky soft and clear, an easy breeze rustling the maples and willows and elms surrounding the pond.

Amos liked holidays. They were monumental events in Macaenas. Not so much because of the holiday and what it celebrated, as for the reason it provided him and others to close up shop without guilt, to relax, spend time with their kids and friends, all without that nagging feeling that they were letting something else slide.

Just before noon, Amos packed a cooler with some beer, sandwiches, macaroni salad, fruit and cheese and snacks, grabbed a lawn chair from the backyard, and headed toward the park. For a moment he considered stopping at Virginia's to see if Delilah wanted to walk over with him, thought she might be more comfortable if she didn't have to go alone. But then he realized she could have gone with Virginia. He hoped she had.

But on Haven Lane he saw Virginia. Alone. Beneath a charming straw hat her full grey hair was tucked up, stray, wiry pieces waving about in the small breeze. She grasped a picnic basket by both hands.

Amos always thought her thin, frail neck seemed too dainty to carry the weight of her hair, but he also loved to see that hair plaited in a single strand down her back as though she were still sixteen. Sometimes it seemed she was.

"Virginia!" he called to her, jogging slowly.

"Amos! Hello! What a nice surprise." They walked together, Virginia on the sidewalk, Amos in the street.

"Can I carry that for you? As always, you look like you cooked for the whole town!"

Virginia laughed, a trill that defied the passing years, retaining a sound reminiscent of pigtails and jump-ropes. "Hardly! That's okay, I'm fine. But it's kind of you to offer."

"I don't think I ever recall seeing you in a hat, Virginia."

She touched a hand to her head as though she just remembered it. "Oh, isn't it wonderful? It would be Delilah's doing, I must admit. I'd forgotten how much I like them."

"Well, it suits you. By the way, where is Delilah? Isn't she coming?"

"She wasn't home when I got up this morning. She's a bit of a wandering soul, that girl. I do hope she comes, though."

"So do I."

"She's just going to need some time." She paused, forcing Amos to do the same. "I've been struggling with something. Something I believe was shared in confidence but... well..."

"What is it?"

"I feel like I'm betraying her, but I think it's important to know."

"Who? Delilah?"

At the sound of the girl's name Virginia shook her head in disbelief. It remained so difficult to comprehend. "She broke down recently. Oh, Amos. What a nightmare. That poor girl --her mother committed suicide in front of her when she was nine years old."

"Oh my god." Amos felt sick. "Good god." The scars he thought he'd seen came clear now. Became real.

"Please don't say anything. I just thought you should know."

"No. Of course not. How did her mother do it?"

"She drowned herself."

Amos closed his eyes, not wanting to know any more. "Jesus, Virginia, what kind of world do we live in?"

"We both know the answer to that, don't we?"

"Remind me."

"Unpredictable. Not always kind."

"Apparently."

"But not always *un*kind, either. Yes?"

Amos smiled in spite of himself. "I know. I know. But -- goddamn!"

"Yup. I know."

They continued walking in silence, waiting for the heaviness to slough off in the breeze. Amos thought of mentioning the scars -- surely Virginia had seen them -- but wasn't sure he really wanted to talk about them. About what they meant.

Finally Virginia paused again, one hand coming to rest on Amos' arm, "By the way, I want to thank you for holding that pie for me the other day."

Amos smiled, thankful for the shift in conversation. "You don't have to thank me. I'm happy to do it. You know that." He guided her across the street, noticing for the first time how the lines around her eyes had deepened. But they were laugh lines, so perhaps it was good.

"Well, I made a dinner that just had to have apple pie after, but I simply wasn't feeling up to it. That happens a lot these days I'm afraid." As in a sleight-of-hand, a subtle misdirection to draw his attention away from her last comment lest he dwell too long upon it, she smoothed non-existent wrinkles from her tan, baggy pants. Never in a dress, always in shirts and men's-cut trousers, Virginia as a perpetual contradiction of youth and age, delicate and strong. She could withstand a tempest by bending to its will. He admired her.

Women often contained more colors, moods and variants than nearly any other natural force, and while that cacophony made them intriguing, if left unattended it could whirl around on itself into a devastating tornado. But Virginia had found a rare kind of balance that accepted everything, rejected nothing, and yet

76

reconciled all of it into a kind of inner peace that was enviable.

"All the more reason to hold one for someone I'm fond of." Amos finally replied as they continued into the park.

"Well, you're a sweet man, Amos. Don't think I haven't noticed you keeping an eye out for me. I appreciate it." Virginia's husband, Carl, had run the body shop across from Amos' store and the two men had become good, solid friends. Even with the nearly twenty years between them. Carl had an easy, even-tempered quality that suggested a depth of wisdom and seemed to bridge the age gap so that Amos never felt Carl to be much older than himself. It left Amos feeling a little responsible for Virginia now. Another reason he was happy Delilah had moved in at her place. "Between you and Delilah," Virginia finished, "I haven't a care in the world."

Amos smiled and kissed Virginia on the forehead.

Crossing the grass in the park and nearing the pond, they finally found two spots near one another in the gathering crowd. Amos set down his cooler and chair, and Virginia found a space for her basket. She took his large, soft hand in hers—smaller, with skin like sheer onion skin—and squeezed it lightly before turning back toward her basket a few people away. "And you come on over here and get some of my potato salad!" she called behind her, making Amos smile. She took care of him as well. Virginia was a good woman. Just about as good as they come. It was probably for the best that Carl went first. He wouldn't have been able to live without her.

In fact, Amos knew all too well how that felt. Being left behind. He'd been privy for the last eighteen months. There was no sunrise, nor dusk, no breath throughout the day that did not carry with it a desperate need to understand how he could have lost his love, his partner, his friend, his delicate connection to the world, so very early in life. But that was the way the disease worked. It was as though one day Ellen was fine, and the next her tawny, mulatto skin turned pale, her soft, full body thinned to helplessness as the cancer engulfed her ovaries, her spirit and her life. And in a heartbeat she was gone.

Every single waking moment of the past year and a half had been filled with his quiet, painful struggle to find a reason, and a way, to go on.

Sometimes that reason came as a comforting breeze through the window in the early morning. Sometimes the fact that everyone who came to his lunch counter knew his name gave him breath for another hour or another day. And sometimes the ability simply sprang from his fear of death being greater than his fear of life without her.

And that is when he would hear Ellen, easily, lightly, full of love and laughter, "Whatever gets you through the day, Amos. Whatever gets you through the day."

He missed her.

"Do I have to stand here all day, or are you going to ask me to join you?"

Amos' head cleared out of the past and focused on Delilah, in sunhat (but with her hair down this time in a single, fiery braid) and sundress, looking much like a cross between a girl playing dress-up and a 1930's starlet. Either one she carried charmingly.

"Why, I'd be honored." Amos gestured to the space beside him as a knight making way for a princess. Delilah spread a blanket out in front of the chair, waved hello to Virginia, kicked off her sneakers and sat cross legged on the ground, her dress billowing out around her like a rayon/cotton cloud. Not a princess. Just a girl. One with a past he now knew a little more of, although he tried not to show it.

"So, is this everyone in town?" She asked him, her head tilted up toward him, her hand shielding the sun from her eyes.

Amos glanced around him before settling into his chair, the joints creaking a bit under his weight. The librarian, Katie Harnett, sat with her husband, Lou; Millie sat with Sarah Martinson who owned the craft store; Ed Carrolton and his wife, Karen; Terry, and the crew from the produce market; the Connors, who owned a farm just past the cemetery—all around him gathered familiar, laughing faces in shirt sleeves and spring dresses. Even a hat or two could be spotted throughout the small crowd. "I guess it's pretty close. 'Though it's still early. There are some who won't show, never do."

"Really? People actually find themselves able to resist the lure of the 'Great Gatherings of the Macaenas Masses'? Or do you folks have some secrets hidden away?" She scanned the people milling around the park, how they laughed, touched arms, or exchanged hugs, wondering what it would be like to know them all by name. She wondered what it would've been like to grow up in this town.

Amos glanced at her then, as her gaze tripped around the crowd, just looking, seeing, with no apparent agenda or purpose, and he realized he could never be sure whether she was being serious or sarcastic. He suddenly realized that's just how it was with Delilah.

You could never be quite sure.

Save for a ten-minute interlude of passing clouds that looked like they might gather enough strength for a shower but failed, the afternoon maintained its perfection, lulling everyone into comfortable serenity.

But Delilah grew restless just before dusk. Shadows grew long, filling in the empty spaces of light between people like blood oozing from a wound, and she could no longer see faces clearly. The crowd became an unknowable creature capable of hiding secrets.

She felt certain she was being watched, her skin prickly, the hair on her neck bristling. The friendly faces of Macaenas seemed to shift and alter, and the wide expanse of the park began to creep inward.

Delilah rocked gently against the rising wave of panic, fingering the hem of her dress, turning toward anyone who passed close by, picking at grass and building little piles on the blanket. "Shit," she said, a little louder than she intended. She had a knot in her stomach.

"Delilah? You okay?" Amos had been watching silently, and after the news Virginia shared of Delilah's past, he had a newfound concern.

"Fine..." she answered too quickly, jumping to her feet. "I just can't sit still for so long." She smiled nervously -- the first time Amos had ever seen her force a smile. "I'm just -- I'm going to take a walk."

Amos considered trying to convince her otherwise, afraid something was seriously wrong, but all he managed was, "Well, we'll be here if you decide to come back."

He watched as she wound her way delicately around picnic blankets and lawn chairs, smiling skittishly to those she passed, occasionally stopping to briefly, tensely chat—but obviously needing to be an arm's length from those around her until she got to the road, her hat a big, peach halo in the late afternoon as she turned left into the woods.

And it was that same peach halo that caught his attention later on as the last of the fireworks catapulted skyward almost simultaneously, the furious explosions lighting the sky nearly as bright as day.

She stood far off to the side at the very edge of the woods partially hidden by a birch tree, one hand holding her hat as she tipped her head back to watch the swirling sparks of arcing light raining down toward the earth.

Had she been there all along?

Why hadn't she just stayed with him?

For all her genuine warmth with others, Delilah remained fiercely private. As though too much too close created an excess of clutter, too much for her to discern the goodness, to find enjoyment. And, of course, to feel safe and secure.

In truth, Amos understood that more than Delilah knew.

Since his childhood he'd felt more comfortable in an uncluttered, unfettered space — both externally and internally. But for him it had meant isolation behind a self-imposed wall that ultimately left him weaker rather than stronger.

So at that moment he envied her strength in standing alone. He only hoped that it was, indeed, her need for solitude and not fear or separateness or some other private darkness that drove her to stand alone at the edge of the woods.

*A*mos felt nostalgic. He left the house one warm Thursday evening and strolled around the quiet streets of town.

When he was a boy, Macaenas was little more than farm country with a small, unassuming stretch of road that served as the main part of town. In summer months, when the air grew heavy and thick, the sweet aroma of manure and hay would creep in from surrounding farms, converging in the center of town and hanging stubbornly in the air like cheap perfume. Movies were a quarter, and the ice cream sodas at the drug store/five-and-dime took what was left of small allowances after Saturday afternoon double features in Sinclair.

He had been a shy, solitary child, his wrinkled brain full of questions and wonders, his bedroom a stockpile of rock, bug, and leaf collections. Smarter than the average resident of Macaenas, he asked intricate questions of the world, demanded complex answers in return, and would have gone on to college had his father not gotten so ill that Amos needed to remain to help with the farm. It was different then. Families were tighter, obligations stronger, bonds fiercer. Or maybe it was only him; as much as he'd discovered the world to be made up of infinite shades of grey, some things remained—at least for him—clearly black and white.

His 'reward' for staying on came in winter less than two years later when, on their way home from a rare night of dinner in Sinclair, his parents' car skidded beneath the trailer of a milk truck that jack-knifed on a patch of ice, the car's windshield shattering, the roof collapsing, just as the two halves of the semi slammed shut, squashing the car like a fly in a book, spilled milk running a river into surrounding snowbanks. It was the worst accident in a decade, the papers reported, and Amos received condolences from people he'd never even met.

After that he sold the farm to a young family looking to build a simple, quiet future and could have gone off on his own adventure, but by then Macaenas had taken root within him, and for so many reasons, he no longer yearned to leave.

So he took the money from the farm and did the opposite of what everyone expected; he bought the store, by then an empty, unused shell, and he stayed.

Now, a lifetime later, as he wandered near the edge of the Carver's Park pond in the fading light, he found Delilah. Knees drawn up near her chest, arms wrapped around her jean-clad legs, chin resting on knee caps, as the intermittent flash of lightning bugs winked patterns around her, She sat on a large, flat stone before a clutch of cattails.

With her eyes closed and her body swaying nearly imperceptibly in tandem with the faint breeze, she nearly vanished into her surroundings, her edges soft and uncertain in the fading twilight. She could have been no more than a wisp, a reflection in dusky fog, a ghost.

Amos nearly left her to her solitary communing, but something told him she wouldn't mind if he sat in the grass beside her. Sometimes it seemed there was as much of himself in Delilah as though she were his own daughter.

She made no move as he approached, although seemed well aware of his presence, nor as he lowered himself to the ground—not quite as gracefully as when he was a child—and took a deep breath of the sweet, heady perfume of honeysuckle and clover that grew in the surrounding field. It reminded him of rolling down hills as a child, arms tucked across his chest, the world a spinning cascade of blurred colors, the dizziness making him giddy.

"You've found my favorite place as a boy." He spoke into the soft twilight.

"You grew up here, Amos?" She answered him with no hint of surprise at his arrival, as though she had expected him all along.

"Yup. That I did. And I spent most of my childhood prowling around this pond."

"Really? I didn't know there were any who actually grew up here. I thought Macaenas was a place people ended up in when they had nowhere else in particular to go." She kept her eyes closed as she talked, only raising or knitting eyebrows showing him any response. What did she see in the dark place behind her eyes? Was there another world in there? Did she travel far? Or was she, really, just half an arm's length away.

"Is that a fact?" His heart skipped. "And so is that why *you're* here?"

She turned to him then, empty eyes, and a sad, sweet smile playing across her face. "Oh, Amos, do *any* of us know why we are here?"

"I do. I grew up here." He returned her smile and added a small challenge to it as he tossed a small pebble into the pond. It made a soft 'plunk'.

"Yes. So you said. Well, good for you, then."

"I'd come here and lay on my stomach at the edge and sink my hands into the shallows trying to catch minnows and crayfish, watching the sun cast rippling shadows on the bottom." He stopped, aware of his uninvited sharing.

Delilah felt the sudden halt, felt his discomfort sitting between them as if it were her own and opened her eyes. "Go ahead. I like listening to you. Why the pond?"

Amos stared into the growing darkness. "I guess because there was so much to explore. I taught myself the different varieties of lichen and rocks and bugs. I spent whole afternoons watching the red wing blackbirds build nests along the shore, learning their calls and songs. I didn't realize it then, but the natural world is an expert teacher. Learning about the pond, discovering its moods, its cycles and the cycles of the life within it, taught me..." He stopped again, feeling foolish.

"What?"

"Well, I think it helped me understand my own life. To accept things like my parents' death, for instance, by teaching me it isn't always necessary to ask why but rather to accept certain things simply because they are."

"But I think sometimes you have to ask 'why', don't you?"

Amos only heard the words of the question because he became flooded, lost, overcome.

He brought Ellen to the pond when they first met, he shy and uncertain, she laughing and childlike, and when she began walking the edge of the pond, pointing out flowers and birds, "Did you know that the Queen Anne's Lace is a wild carrot? Look at the root!", like he was one of her elementary students. He fell instantly in love with her. The sun seemed to choose specific strands of hair to highlight, and her eyes so sparkled that he imagined they might refract the light perfectly enough to create a rainbow inside her skull.

And when they perched on the rocks beside the pond as the sun went down, picking out constellations and making first-starlight-wishes, she in turn fell in love with him. His quiet nature, rooted strength, his loneliness.

Through their long talks by that pond, Ellen coaxed him out of his solitary world, teaching him the safety of held hands and shared tears. And on the same night, he found the strength to breathe the words, "I love you," as they watched the sunset reflected in the water—in that very same breath he also --

"I proposed to Ellen here." He whispered to the fireflies.

"When I was a child," Delilah spoke as though they had been in unbroken conversation, aware his last comment was not meant for her, "I saw things—light and shadows around people and objects that made me think of ideas and places I can't fully recall now and am not certain were ever real. Like dreaming and then not being sure if you had dreamed it or lived it.

"At night in bed I'd lay half in and half out of sleep and the darkness around me became full of its own kind of light. It wasn't just blackness, but rather hues of deepness, all possessing their own glow, but too dense for the ordinary eye to see. I felt I had fallen out of the ordinary world and into something—well, extraordinary. It became alive, the darkness, painting trees and people and grass—everything—with a kind of... phosphorescence. You'd think it would have scared the pants off me, but it was so beautiful, Amos. Everything around me had life. Everything—pulsed. It made me feel I wasn't quite alone. Made me feel that, in the end, we are more than what we see of each other every day.

"Now I catch glimpses of it from time to time, brief flashes out of the corner of my eye, but not much. I can only remember the sense of it. The vastness and enormity of how it made me feel.

"There is so very much more to this world than what we can see with our eyes, Amos. I'm certain of it."

And she turned back toward the darkness as it sank deeper over the pond, the field, and their two figures sitting alone together at the border between the two.

That night sleep eluded Amos.

It remained just out of reach, like a glimmer in the corner of your eye, a shadow, a wraith that vanishes when you turn to face it head on.

In his living room, awash in the flickering light of the T.V., he gripped the remote and endlessly flipped through the gamut of channels.

In the bedroom he paced a track in front of the windows, in the kitchen he stood before the open refrigerator; room to room he traveled, fingering dust, scanning books, staring at the sky, his slippers, the wall, as though sleep could be hiding somewhere nearby.

It wasn't until he gave up, opened a beer, and stretched out in the overstuffed chair in the bedroom that sleep finally snuck up on him, stealing in through the shadows, lulling him into dreams.

The Fourth of July fireworks seemed to have sparked off the summer heat; cicadas buzzing throughout sticky afternoons, nights weighing heavily and travelling slowly, and Amos heard air conditioners and fans humming in almost every window as he made his way from his house on Ellington Street to the store on Main early Friday morning. So early, in fact, it had barely ceased to be night.

His boots made a soft, heavy sound on the narrow sidewalk like a basketball dropped on grassy earth. No other sounds interrupted, and for an instant he felt a sense of space, a comforting insignificance, as though he was completely alone on the planet.

He wasn't, of course, alone on the planet, or in his early rising, because he knew at the Connor's—and other farms—breakfast dishes were already cleaned and dried, and the first chores of the day had begun.

The produce market would be the next to awaken, trucks rumbling through the early dawn bringing fresh corn and peaches and deep green spinach beaded with spring water, until finally, like a chain of dominoes, lights would flip on all across town and the day would finally, officially begin.

The lights were already on in the Emmett kitchen, Virginia probably making muffins or cookies for Delilah to take to work. "You're too thin!" he'd witnessed Virginia say, poking Delilah gently in the ribs.

There was no reason for Amos to rise so early save that he loved to be alone in the darkness of the store, pies warming in the oven, the aroma of spiced apples and sweet cherries mixing with the rich, dense fragrance of the first coffee of the day, most of the world still wrapped in quiet slumber.

Even Millie's cat, Rufus—who spent the nights prowling the neighborhood—lay belly up on her front lawn as he passed, lulled by the gentle shift from night to morning, only the tip of his tail twitching in the fading darkness.

It seemed a magic time, the world free of prior sins, pureness possible, if only for a moment.

By the time Amos reached the store, a thin line of golden peach tinted the horizon beyond the pond, leaves shone as though dipped in rose gold, and already the thermometer hanging by the soda machine outside the door read seventy-five degrees. It would be a day worth little more than iced-teas and air conditioning. He took off his Red Sox baseball cap to wipe the sweat from his forehead, as Terry, the manager at the open market, drove by and waved. Amos, returning the cap to his head, reached for the key clip on his belt loop, every motion coming slowly, tiredly, the humidity already so high it felt as though his body weight had doubled. Maybe he was just getting old, but he couldn't recall these summer days taking a toll on him as a boy — all-day bike rides and baseball games were never hampered by heat. But today he took three steps and needed to sit down in the shade. The truly hot days — dog days — of August were still a few weeks away; yet if it was this hot already, he didn't want to know what the following month would bring.

"'Morning, Amos." Delilah appeared from around the corner of the building, her voice softer than usual. Amos jumped and dropped his keys, which hit the pavement with a dull, hard ring. "Sorry. I didn't take you for a man quite that easy to startle." She leaned against the corner of the store, the rising sun just beginning to glow golden-orange on her skin. The effect on her copper hair was unearthly.

Amos stared a moment at the keys glinting in the sunlight and made the long descent to where they lay, unhappy about the involuntary groan that came with the push back to standing. "Yeah, well, don't let this bearish physique fool you. I'm very sensitive. What the hell are you doing up so early?" He hadn't realized it until that exact moment, when he paused to look Delilah in the eye, the green of them luminescent in the sun, that he had dreamed of Ellen all night long.

"You're not the only one who has dreams, you know." Amos froze. Did she really know about his dreams? Could she? Or was it just that his glassy, heavy eyes told the same tale as hers? Perhaps it was more than summer heat and age weighing him down.

"I couldn't sleep," Delilah went on, "so I didn't. I've been spending the early hours watching Virginia's morning glories open—but it happens so slowly! Did you know that? Just small increments of movement so slow you can't see them happening. Suddenly, they're open."

Suddenly he was glad for Delilah's company.

"Having bad dreams, are you?" He slid the key in the lock and opened the door. "Want to talk about them?"

"Can't remember them, I'm afraid." She squinted at him in the growing sunlight, at his eyes lined with faint furrows, a thin trail of sweat leaking down his temple. He seemed somehow needful, suddenly aging, becoming unreachable. All at once she felt like crying.

"Hmm... care to come in and keep me company anyway?"

Delilah followed wordlessly behind and took her seat at the counter. Either melancholy was in the air, thus explaining Amos' somber mood, or she had brought it with her, unintentionally infecting him. She hoped against the latter, even though her "sulky moods" had been pointed out to her in the past as something with the power to ruin another's day. It made her guilty about her moods. Anger, sadness, confusion—anything other than contentment carried along a measure of guilt. *I'll give you something to be upset about!* The voice flooded her brain, a cold, stinging tidal wave. It reminded her of the sleeplessness night, full of voices, pressure building in her ears as though the altitude had changed.

"Coffee?" He flipped on the air conditioning which whirred to life and quickly settled to a steady hum.

Startled, Delilah looked up. "Please, yes. I could use a cup right about now." She worked a smile from her lips as she rubbed a bit of Macaenas dust from her eye and tried to settle skittish nerves.

"More like sleep is what you could use." Amos spoke with his back turned as he filled the coffee machine.

Delilah flipped her hand through the air dismissively, feigning an aristocratic air. "Terribly overrated, sleep. We waste one third of our lives doing it. People do far too much of it."

"And some people do far too little."

"Don't need it. Don't want it. In fact, I may never sleep again." She spun around on her stool watching the walls of the store whirl by her, booths bleeding to shelves, bleeding to register, to Amos, to window, to booth... forcing giddiness to rise.

"Well, now that seems a bit extreme, don't you think? By the way, I noticed Virginia is up already. In

93

case you want to give her a call so she knows you aren't there."

"She knows." A moment of silence passed between them, the coffee pot perking and spitting, the sunlight sneaking its way across the counter top in a slant that sought to engulf first the napkin holder, then the salt shaker, and the world, as both Amos and Delilah became temporarily lost in private thoughts.

When her stool slowed to a stop and the world ceased its whirling, Delilah fingered the salt and pepper shakers, placing them in a line with the other containers on the counter. "Did you know," she began, "that in many tribal cultures people believe dreams are actually journeys to another world?"

He did know, and he said so.

"Do you believe that, Amos? That in some ways our dreams are real?" She paused with her hand on the sugar container.

"To be honest, I've never really thought about it, although it wouldn't surprise me to find out there was some truth to it."

Delilah smiled briefly and turned her attention back to the sugar, unable to find a suitable place for it. "It seems possible, I suppose. I mean, how do we know this world isn't a dream? How do we know that this isn't the dream and when we sleep we're actually returning to the 'real world'? She finally slid the sugar between the napkin holder and the salt shaker and looked Amos square in the eye. In her mind, vague nightmares drifted — dark rooms full of shadows and unseen hands reaching out from invisible corners.

Amos stood silently a moment, absorbing Delilah and the curious wonderings of her mind. "Well, Delilah, you aren't the first to ponder that question, that's for certain. And I can tell you that going down that road can drive you just a little bit nuts." He smiled.

"But what if it were true?"

It wasn't hard for Amos to call up a few of his dreams and imagine how he'd feel if they were real. "Sometimes I think that would be just fine. How about you?"

"I think it's pretty much the same either way." Delilah smiled at him then and covered a huge yawn with the back of her right hand. "So, how about that coffee? Before I pass out at your counter? That wouldn't be very good for business." She flashed a smile.

Amos smiled in return, poured her a cup of coffee and put in two sugars. *The same either way.* He wished that were true for him.

She took a deep drink of the coffee, pausing as though allowing the wash of it to baptize her. Renew her. "Oh, Amos, no one can make a cup of coffee like you."

"Flattery will get you everywhere, young lady." He had to turn away after he spoke, suddenly feeling his words weighing heavily in the air, pressing down on the soft tissue below his ribcage. Not because of Delilah, who simply grinned warmly at him, as always, but from himself, suddenly so empty. It caught him off guard, but he shook the feeling away as nothing more than residual melancholy from his dreaming of Ellen.

He winced. Just the sound of her name echoing in his mind carried pain.

"You miss her all of the time, don't you?"

She caught him off guard again—too many times for so early in the day—and he had to sit down on a stool he kept tucked behind the counter. How did she know? He felt a rush of ice water through his veins. Was this girl a witch? Psychic? Gifted in the ways of the otherworld? How did she know about Ellen?

Delilah read the panicked, bewildered look on Amos' face and smiled, nodding to a framed photograph sitting beside the cash register. "Virginia told me. I'm sorry if I've broken a confidence or intruded in any way."

Amos felt a hundred years old in a way that made him yearn not for youth, but for death. He scratched at his ear. "What made you say that I miss her all the time?" He tried not to look too weary, but he knew it didn't work.

"Oh, it's obvious, really. At least it is to me. That sadness. Aloneness. Particularly when I noticed you meandering around the house at some ungodly hour last night. It was the walk of the heavy-hearted." She hadn't meant to let it slip. That she had watched him.

Amos stared at her. At her radiant hair, and her soft pure skin, and eyes that were both childish and ancient at the same time. He nearly laughed, though more out of nervousness than amusement. The more he knew her, the less he seemed to know. "You aren't going to tell me that you have any reason to know that kind of walk, are you?" He caught a look in her that revealed just how tired she was and how hard she was fighting it. She seemed to carry thoughts far too weighty, and the energy it took to own such thoughts, such feelings, such depth of knowledge, was draining.

"Nope. As a matter of fact, I'm not going to tell you anything. What do you think about that?" She cocked one eyebrow playfully, trying to fight the painful squeeze in her heart.

"Hrm. Not quite the answer I was looking for at all."

"Well then, you should be more careful with your questions!" She rose from her stool and started to reach into the pocket of her jeans. The pressure in the store seemed to suddenly rise and Delilah felt her lungs tighten; she needed to leave before it crushed her skull.

"If you're fishing for money to pay for that coffee, forget it," Amos said. "It's on the house. For the company and for chasing away the shadows."

"My pleasure, Amos. Always my pleasure."

She disappeared out the door into a blasting ray of early morning sunshine that promised to set the world on glorious, purifying fire.

As soon as Delilah was clear of the door and out of Amos' view, she ran.

She ran hard past a handful of boys outside the news stand, stolen cigarettes cupped in their ten year old hands; past Harold slowly lumbering down Main Street, an armload of books cradled before him; across the parking lot behind the long-closed Emmet's gas station; then hard across Raven Road, where she stumbled on the curb, twisting her ankle; to the stretch of meadow on the other side full of wheat grass and goldenrod and into the thicket of woods beyond. She ran through the underbrush, brambles and burrs clinging to her socks and her shirt, and up the rocky incline of the hills, pushing complaining muscles, leaping fallen trees and gullies until she came out the other side of the woods on a peak of the hill overlooking the railroad tracks.

There she stopped, collapsing on a small log on the edge of the hill, her heart pounding, her lungs straining, her pulse thundering in her temples -- and she cried. Tears full of sorrow and confusion and unanswered rage that will consume from the inside out if it is left to fester.

She cried for Amos and his long nights of dark loneliness. She cried for herself and for all things gone, never to be recovered, and she cried for a world full of empty, lost souls, with hearts left fragile by hurt or loss, but too frightened to admit it, to reach out to one another and hold on.

Hold on.

Hold on there, girl! Where do you think you're headed?

The voice slammed against the inside of her head, and she clasped her hands over her ears as though afraid the force of it might kick a hole in her skull. She squeezed her eyes shut trying to force out the memory, the man, the nightmare -- the inescapable, immutable, eternal truths of her life before. And when the train came speeding by, blowing its whistle into the quiet, clear morning, Delilah raised her voice along with it as loud and long as she could until her breathlessness dissolved into fits of uncertain laughter, as though all the demons that had nestled within her throughout the night had been cast out on her primal, mournful howl. Exorcised. Or perhaps they had just driven her mad. She wasn't sure she cared which it was. Then she fell back on a patch of grass, watching pale wisps of clouds, vaporous, sheer curtains draped over a palette of pure blue. Lulled by their diaphanous drifting, she closed her eyes.

If there could be no peace, perhaps, at least, there could be rest.

Perhaps.

As the echo of the train died a slow, trailing death in the distance, Harold stood silent and unseen behind an oak tree, index finger mindlessly twirling a lock of his hair, his eyes sad and dark, while his lips soundlessly mouthed a single word.

Delilah.

Millie sat at Amos' counter for an uncharacteristic cup of pre-lunch coffee later that morning, and other Macaenans rustled around the store chatting idly, looking for any kind of distraction. Amos figured the heat made people restless. It dropped low into the valley, molding to the contours of the hills until there seemed no room to move, no air to breathe.

"Good morning, Amos."

Amos was surprised to see Virginia, and eyed her curiously as she perched a small basket on the corner of the counter near the cash register.

"Well, good morning to you, Virginia! What a pleasant surprise! What brings you here today?"

"Well, to be honest," She paused, glancing to others nearby, lowering her voice. "Do you have a minute?"

"For you? Always."

Setting the basket on the counter, Virginia motioned to the back office.

Amos followed behind her. "Is everything okay?" he asked.

Virginia shut the door behind them. "Delilah mentioned to me that she felt you were having a bit of a tough time lately. I hope you don't mind me bringing it up." She absently rubbed at her elbow. She felt a fatigue in her arms that was new. *Bone tired*, her mother used to call it.

Amos knit his brow. "No, not at all. She's quite perceptive, that Delilah."

"And I have to apologize. She noticed that photo of you and Ellen and asked me about it. It wasn't really my place, I know..."

"It's okay."

"I just worry..."

"It's okay, Virginia. Really." And although it truly was okay with him that Virginia had shared his story, he also had a feeling that something had been set in motion, something big.

"Well, it isn't much, really," Virginia continued, "but I know you've always been fond of my apple muffins, so I brought you over a bunch. Comfort food." Amos returned her smile and looked at his shoes. They were old, the leather cracking where it creased at his toes. "And if you ever need anything, Amos—all you have to do is call. We've been friends a long time."

Glancing out the window over Virginia's shoulders he felt closer to tears than he had in a long, long while.

But he fought them. He had no place for them. "Thank you, Virginia. Thank you very much." He heard a car horn outside, then the timer in the kitchen rang, and his pulse throbbed in his ears. As a child, when pressures grew too intense, he'd climb to the top of a maple tree in their backyard and look out over their roof at nothing in particular. He didn't have a maple tree now. Instead he reached for the door.

Virginia caught his hand. "I mean it, Amos. We've both lost a lot in our lives. I know what it can do to you. You don't have to feel it all alone. If Delilah's given me one thing, it's that." She had thought Amos was coming back from Ellen's death, finding some sort of closure and comprehension, but through Delilah's eyes she began to notice a dark silence in him. And a painfully closed heart. She knew the feeling, knew its colors and sounds and smells and how it seemed to fall inward on you with each passing breath.

"There are things some people know nothing about," Virginia spoke again, "loneliness is one. Some folks live their whole lives without feeling loneliness. Not because they aren't lonely, but because they never stop long enough to actually feel it. They never sit, alone in a room, listen to the silence, and feel the loneliness. They're too scared. But that usually means they don't feel much else, either.

"Delilah's not one of those people. In fact, she's just the opposite. I'll bet she's spent most of her young life sitting alone in a room living in her loneliness. That's what makes her so sensitive to that feeling in others. That's what draws her to you and me."

101

Amos appeared puzzled. "I don't know, Virginia. I never really thought I was lonely. *Alone*, yes. But not lonely. Not really." A dull ache had begun growing in the middle of his forehead as though something was trying to get out.

Virginia smiled. "That's because for the last year and half you've been moving so fast away from your pain that you create your own wind. But Delilah saw it. And now that you're slowing down, you're seeing it too. Aren't you?"

Amos couldn't speak. He didn't dare. He only squeezed Virginia's hand and nodded before leaving the office and returning to the counter.

He didn't see Virginia as she watched him quietly a moment and then turned to leave.

Losing a love was painful even after a lifetime together. Virginia couldn't fathom losing one so young.

Delilah was already sitting on the iron bench outside the hat store when Millie arrived to open up. She sat slouched down, her head against the curved back of the bench, eyes closed, a dull throbbing at the base of her skull. The kind you get after a deep, therapeutic cry. She could still feel the heat of that cry behind her eyes.

She had so relaxed into the shape and feel of the bench that it appeared she'd been there all night. Maybe longer. Maybe her whole life.

"Morning, Delilah! You're here early today." Millie unlocked the gate in front of the door and slid it to the side, peeking at Delilah over the top of her black, cat's-eye sunglasses.

"Mmm. Just restless, I guess." Delilah's voice came small and quiet causing Millie to pause before sliding the key into the door.

"You okay, honey? You look tired."

"Do I? Well, I didn't sleep very well last night, I guess."

"Oh, well, nobody does in this heat. Gotta give your body time to adjust. That's all." She unlocked the door and went inside.

"Hm. Yeah." Delilah remained on the bench, her face turned toward the sun. It seeped into her pores, ran long, thin channels through her body — tiny strings of comforting heat traversing through limbs, lungs, heart. She breathed deeply.

"You coming, Delilah?" Millie called over her shoulder before she let the door close.

"Yup. I'm coming," Delilah muttered. But she still sat, unmoving, her upturned face awash in golden, summer sun. "Just need a little more time."

Way out on Route One, almost another state away, Jeff McNeely was at the tail-end of his shift at the 7-11. He watched an old, pea-green Dodge Dart with a missing rear bumper peel off the highway into the parking lot, its sudden turn filling the oppressive air with the stench of burning rubber.

From the driver's side emerged a middle-aged man, several days growth of beard obscuring what could, on other occasions be described as a distinguished, square jaw. In fact, with a shower, shave and even one square meal he might clean up into a responsible looking, slim, greying-at-the-temples older man. But at the moment, he just slipped into the store for two six-packs of cheap beer, Jeff noticing his red-rimmed eyes looking glassy and unfocused as the guy mumbled incoherently before skulking back to the car, tripping once over the curb.

An hour later Jeff finished his shift, and as he walked outside, he noticed that the Dart was still parked, the guy passed out in the driver's seat, six empty cans and an empty bottle of scotch strewn on the seat beside him.

The heat worked on everyone like a timed-release sedative, lulling them into a sedentary, still afternoon.

Harold sat on the curb outside Virginia's, watching a horsefly slowly go insane on the sidewalk, alternately skipping and buzzing along the cement, then flipping over on its back, legs akimbo, wings shuddering.

Lunch was slow for Amos.

He stood behind the counter with one foot on a shelf beside extra creamers and packs of napkins. Arms crossed on his knee, he leaned forward and stared outside.

The heat was almost visible; the sky looked thick and white — like pure, hot light. In the stagnant air the awning peeking down into view hung motionless and even the wasps that made their home in the eave over the front window were still.

Just the steady hum of the air conditioner droning hard against the temperature outside — white noise to go with the white light.

Still and quiet.

All that stillness created a vacuum into which all the nagging issues of Amos' life suddenly tumbled, filling his mind with things he preferred to avoid. Things he thought he'd already settled.

Things.

Ellen. His life. Time, Ellen, God, Ellen, Ellen, Ellen.

Yes. He missed her all the time.

All the time.

Time.

How can there be too much of it and not enough of it simultaneously?

It seemed that prior to Delilah's arrival he had at least begun to draw some closure and find a way to move beyond the grief and loss and anger.

Now he feared perhaps he'd only fooled himself into believing he'd done so, when all he'd actually accomplished was an effective way to disregard it all in a manner that mimicked closure and healing. In which case he wasn't sure there was enough time in the life of the entire universe to find closure and move on.

He rubbed the back of his neck and stifled a surge of tears. He rubbed his eyes and paced behind the counter. He poured a cup of coffee which then grew cold beside the register.

Once he'd thought you could step forward and leave things behind forever, but you can't. You always have to go back to it, whatever it is, because if it happened, if it existed, it's a part of you. So unless you find a way to run away from *yourself*, you're stuck with it.

You and it—whatever it is—are the same creature. And some wounds go too deep.

*J*uly wound its way slowly toward the heat-drenched days of August in the same quiet, lazy way as always. Huge, slow bumblebees ambled their furry way from lupine to lavender, tiny wings beating frantically to hold their hefty bodies aloft. Retrievers, beagles and collies took refuge beneath the cooling shade of elm trees, tongues lolling sideways, waiting for the high, noon sun to lose its grip on the sky and sink lower, where it would cast cooling shadows across wildly growing lawns. Squealing children ran through spinning sprinklers; parents packed their cars with towels and books and money for ice cream, heading out for a day at the Sinclair public pool.

Evenings, the air filled with the sharp aroma of barbecues as children bounced from yard to yard, their faces slick and sticky with watermelon juice.

The sun set slowly, spilling intense, tropical splashes across the sky, electric pink and mango and cranberry lighting the edges of cotton clouds.

Same as always.

But beneath it all, underscoring the sameness like a distant tympani drum, came a faint, discordant hum. A vibration of something stirring.

Out on Route One the green dodge slowed from seventy-five to thirty-five as the driver, Jack Gruffen, eased off the highway and onto the shoulder. He leaned his head back on the seat a moment, his lungs tight, an uncomfortable squeezing around his heart.

He fought for breath, considering for an instant that he might be having a heart attack; it would be just his luck. Then, what he moved to brush off his cheek turned out to be tears. "Shit," he mumbled, fighting the emotion. He'd almost rather the heart attack.

Popping the glove compartment, he retrieved several photographs, two of which caught his attention, the images pressing even harder against his lungs, tightening his throat, forcing a black stain of grief to slide forward from behind him like a shadow sliding across the ground.

The first photo held the image of a woman with long, strawberry-blonde hair woven in a single braid that fell over her shoulder. The picture was old, yellowing, but he could still make out the scattered freckles on her nose below the hand that shielded the sun from her eyes, and the cocky, playful smirk that tilted her lips.

"I loved you... didn't you know that?" he whispered. "I loved you..."

He dropped the photos on the passenger seat before giving any others a second glance. How could the strength of his pain have endured so long? Was it a punishment? For what? Loving someone? In his mind that's all he'd ever done. How could she have done what she did? How?

Deep in his brain the vice began to tighten, sending tiny pinpoints of fiery pain into his temples and behind his eyes. That was how it always began, slowly building, bleeding, radiating out into his limbs, his gut, until it paralyzed him and threatened to drive him mad.

Reaching behind his seat, he grabbed a bottle from the floor, unscrewed the cap which slipped from his hand and vanished somewhere beneath his seat. Gauging the amount left in the bottle he tipped it back, emptied it, and tossed the bottle into the back seat, where it rolled into a corner. Then, grinding the car into gear as the liquor's heat began to melt the pain in his head and obliterate the soft thoughts of longing, he spun back onto the highway hoping the stifling heat and the sharp searing of the alcohol would permanently burn the unwanted memories from his brain.

A beer bottle clamped in his right fist, Amos lay in the hammock in his backyard beneath a half moon cutting through small wisps of clouds as the pale light of stars just began to emerge against the cobalt sky. The fingers of his right hand drummed the bottle, his lips pursed, and he clacked his teeth together. His thoughts, a bundle of nervous, unfocused energy, meandered around the edges of newly-stirred emotions.

When Ellen died, he cried and cursed and damned a world so full of cruelty. He thought the ache—deep and penetrating -- would engulf him and finally consume him. He had prayed that it would.

Yet it appeared to have done little more than scratch the surface of his grieving, as now the full weight and finality of the loss lay upon his heart. It seemed, however ironic, that the full sense of what he'd lost had to solidify completely—crystallize with sharp edges and clear reflections—before it could dissipate, and with solidity came a stream of questions and ruminations.

He began to wonder how his life might have been different had Ellen survived. It was something he'd never allowed himself to consider.

Until now.

Reaching back through thick webs of emotional scar tissue, he recalled the full curve of her hip and how it always ignited his desire for her. While she complained of not being svelte enough, he would watch her move and long for the moments when he could trace the ebb and flow of her shape—when he could hold her by the easy slope of her waist as she crawled astride him when they made love. She had been sensitive and passionate, a fire that could collapse into a fit of girlish giggles in an instant.

She was six years his junior and longed to start a family nearly as soon as they were married. That was how the cancer was discovered. When their world quickly lost its footing.

He tried to imagine what their child would have been like—the little girl he'd yearned for—with his sense of humor and Ellen's confidence, his height and Ellen's eyes, her hair, her pale splash of freckles.

But somehow each time he pictured her, this never-to-be-child, she appeared with long ringlets of red hair, and hazel eyes full of easy laughter and quiet sadness.

He saw Delilah.

Always Delilah.

Delilah of the strange and wonderful.

He stifled a wrenching urge to scream, to let loose the rising tide within him. Instead he leapt from the hammock and hurled his beer bottle at the side of his house, the glass shattering with a pop, sending a nearby ruffed grouse thundering out of the brush into the air.

Then, silence.

"Amos?" Delilah stepped carefully around the corner into the backyard. Amos stood without speaking, without acknowledging her, and so she thought had hadn't heard her. "Amos?"

"Go away, Delilah." Amos' mind was dark, dense, too heavy for him to climb out of just now.

"What is it? Can I..."

"I said go away!" Uncharacteristically, Amos spun on his heel, his fists clenched, the pain in his heart so intense it made his eyes throb. "Go away! Jesus!"

Delilah froze. Every instinct said flee, yet the part of her who recognized the man before her as Amos told her it wasn't necessary.

"I don't fucking get it!" Amos continued, pacing around his yard. "I've been fine! Even if I'm fooling

111

myself, who gives a goddamn rat's ass if it means I can at least pretend to be happy?"

Delilah swallowed, her throat thick and hot. When she spoke, her voice came so small that she wasn't sure she had actually spoken at all. "Please. Don't yell at me."

"Oh shit, Delilah. You know, you probably mean well. In fact, I'm sure you do..." He moved toward her and her stomach knotted, "... but I have to tell you, sometimes you need to just leave people alone. I mean, I don't see *you* volunteering anything about yourself, but you sure as hell demand that I give shit up to you!"

"Please, Amos. God, please don't..."

"LEAVE ME ALONE!"

"AMOS!" Virginia came around the corner of her house to the fence and stopped Amos mid-stride toward Delilah, who felt her knees buckle, sending her collapsing to the ground.

Amos blinked as if struck, the rage leaving his face as he followed Virginia's eye toward Delilah who sat trembling on the ground, eyes wide, staring at an unknown spot before her. "Oh, shit. Shit. I'm sorry." He moved toward her, but she leapt to her feet without ever acknowledging she actually saw him coming and moved back toward the front of the house.

"Delilah..." he tried again. But Virginia stopped him with a motion of her hand.

Delilah never turned her back on Amos, backing and sidestepping her way toward the gate with Amos trailing behind, a puppy with his tail between his legs. She moved quietly, suddenly smaller and lighter, her arms wrapped around her body. She opened the gate and stepped through, then paused after turning to close it behind her. When she looked at Amos, her gaze was vacant, so distant that it instantly reduced him to tears.

She turned toward Virginia's house, leaving Amos struggling for his voice, which drowned in the tears burning behind his eyes and the regret that rose from the bile in his stomach.

In the house, Delilah felt panic radiating outward from her lungs as she imagined the shadows following her, closing in. She raced up the stairs, and once in her room, she locked the door and scanned the space, finally moving to the far left corner where she slid a side chair out of the way and crouched, pressing her back against the wall until her shoulder blades hurt. From that position, she could see the entire room, could see that the shadows remained a safe distance away; from there she hummed a quiet tune to herself, her arms wrapped around her knees, her eyes alert and watching all through the long, quiet night.

When Jack Gruffin nearly drove his dodge dart off the road for the third time that night, he took the next exit and pulled into a gas station.

"Fill 'er up," he told the young man that emerged from the attendant's booth as he pulled up to the pump.

Flipping down the visor Jack glanced at a piece of paper he affixed there with a rubber band. His eyes glossed over the bus numbers and town names for the thousandth time and he matched them to a red line drawn on a map in the passenger seat. He crossed several names off the list.

The attendant appeared at the car window. "That'll be eleven-fifty, please."

Jack dug twelve dollars from his wallet and handed the bills out the window.

"You need directions or anything?" The young man nodded to the map on the passenger seat.

Jack returned his wallet to his pocket. He was tired and thirsty and in no mood for chat. "Did I ask for directions?" He turned a glacial eye in the attendant's direction as he shook a cigarette from his pack.

"Well, no. You didn't. I'll get your change."

"Wait..." Jack put his hand out the window toward the young man –- Billy, he now noticed it said on his overalls. "I'm sorry. I'm just tired. It's hot as hell. Been driving a while. You know?"

"There's a motel just a couple of miles down the road."

Jack tried his best to smile. "Thanks. I appreciate that." He turned the ignition and started the Dodge. "Keep the change."

Delilah did not emerge from her room until the following evening when she appeared in the kitchen for dinner. She sat quietly at first but soon showed no signs of the confrontation, full of animated conversation and laughter. Each time Virginia tried to broach the subject, Delilah waved her away with an, "It's okay. I'm okay."

Virginia didn't quite believe her, but being familiar with people reluctant to open up, she let it be.

"I just don't know why Amos keeps it all shut inside him until it explodes," Virginia mused as she and Delilah washed dinner dishes later that night. The overhead light cast a dim yellow stain over them as most of its glow centered on a wooden fruit bowl on the tiled kitchen table, nectarines and peaches sweetening the air. All around them, beyond the light's reach, corners of the room slowly crept inward with the coming darkness. "I try to get him to talk, to convince him it takes a world of time and lots of help, but any mention of her and he disappears inside himself."

"Amos strikes me as a very private person. He doesn't seem to share *anything* easily. Not even his laughter." Delilah stood by with a towel to dry the dishes Virginia handed her. She liked the feel of the scalloped edges of the dishes and would trace the blue pattern of vines and flowers with her finger. In the silences of their conversation, she tried to recall the incident with Amos that Virginia referred to throughout dinner, but all she saw in her mind were bits of Amos' face contorted in painful anger and a rush of fear in her own heart. Nothing more.

"He wasn't always. Ellen took a lot of him with her when she died. They were so much in love." She smiled, and her fist rapped gently against her heart as though to dislodge a pebble caught within.

"Some things are just impossible to come back from."

Virginia paused in her washing and turned toward Delilah, who stood with an arm outstretched, ready to receive the next dish.

The scar on her wrist stood clearly visible against the otherwise youthful perfection of her skin. It looked like a sad, angry creature that finally prompted her to speak. "Delilah..."

But in that strange way Delilah had of seeming to know another's thoughts, she deflected the conversation, "Of course, if you keep feeding him those apple muffins of yours, I think he'll tell you anything you want to know. In fact, I believe you lace them with some kind of magic. I'm sure Millie would love to know the secret!"

Virginia, caught off guard by the compliment, waved her away, suddenly a shy schoolgirl embarrassed by the praise. "Oh, you get out! They aren't *that* good!"

But the wonderful thing about Virginia, and one of the things Delilah loved about her, was that even though she knew they were that good, she would never say so.

"Actually, they are. And I'll say it to anybody. Virginia's Magic Muffins!" She waved her hand through the air as if placing a banner there.

Bubbles of laughter spilled from Virginia. "Oh! Please. The only possible magic that gets in there is maybe a little dose of love and compassion."

"Never underestimate how far those two things will go, Virginia."

Remembering the scars, Virginia tried again. "Delilah, I want to ask you..."

"And meanwhile," Delilah interjected again, "how often do you talk to him about Carl?"

Something about hearing Delilah say her husband's name, the way it hit the air like a hammer against metal, startled Virginia, demolishing any remaining questions for Delilah. She dropped the bowl she'd been washing and watched it shatter on the blue and white tile floor.

The name seemed to echo throughout the house, catching in scalloped molding and lace curtains where it would remain until an errant breeze, or perhaps a boisterous eruption of unexpected laughter, would one day shake it free.

"Oh!" It came out of her more like a child spotting her first butterfly than an aging woman staring at a broken dish.

"Oh, God, Virginia. I'm sorry." Delilah bent down to pick up the broken pieces.

"Oh, honey, that's okay. It just slipped."

Delilah would not look up, tears filling her eyes. "No No. I don't know what I was thinking. Oh, look. It's smashed."

"It's all right. Delilah..." Virginia took her by the shoulders and raised her to her feet. "Sweetheart, what is it? It's just a dish, honey, forget it."

Delilah cried silently for a while, tears as big as a child's, her deep breaths bringing another string of tears, but not enough strength to speak. All the while she fought the silent shadows taunting her from within. Shadows who all owned the same face—a face she would instantly recognize should it step into the light. But it wouldn't. It lived in the shadows.

Finally, pressing her palms to her eyes until she saw tiny, white sparks and taking a great, steadying breath she looked Virginia in the eye. "If there is one person on this earth I never want to cause any kind of pain, it's you. I should never have mentioned his name."

"Oh, Delilah..."

"No!" Delilah pulled away. "I just don't think sometimes! I'm thoughtless and insensitive—God! What the hell is wrong with me?"

Virginia was stunned, Delilah's reaction so volatile, her words strange, the tone not her own. Stepping forward she wrapped her arms around Delilah who suddenly appeared as fragile and vulnerable as a baby bird. For an instant it seemed to Virginia she could scoop Delilah into her own tired arms and cradle her like an infant—there was no more to the girl than that. "You never cause me pain, honey. Never. You've brought me more joy than I thought I'd ever know again in my lifetime. You are the *most* thoughtful and sensitive person I have ever known and I don't mind talking about Carl. Really. I just—I don't know. I don't ever recall hearing you say his name, and something about the way you said it, or the way I heard it—I don't know. It rang so true that I nearly believed he'd come stomping through the door smelling of motor oil and gasoline. I almost believed he was here." She pulled away and looked Delilah in the eye, wiping a tear she saw there. "But he isn't. And that hurts. Still. But like I said, a person can't bear the deep wounds of life all on their own." She cupped Delilah's chin in her hand and briefly, unobtrusively, brushed her fingers across the scar on Delilah's wrist. Just a quick touch that might have been inadvertent, but wasn't. "You remember that."

At ten years of age, Delilah lay in the emergency room behind a drawn curtain as a young intern plastered her left wrist. Beyond the curtain, in the hallway, she

118

could hear her father's voice rising and falling, although the words themselves did not register -- just the sound: harsh, tense, brief.

When the doctor came in to see her again, asking the same question he'd asked a half dozen times since she was brought in, she answered, again, "I'm kind of a klutz. I fell."

She heard the doctor and the intern discuss her demeanor. They commented on her calmness, her lack of response to pain that must have been excruciating considering the bone of her forearm had been protruding through her skin when her father rushed her in. But they didn't understand. There was no pain. There was just blackness. Emptiness. She was no longer even in the bed in the hospital, but rather floating, disconnected, in some ethereal halfway house—detached from the chaos around her, alone, untouched, safe.

When the dishes were done, instead of wandering off as was her habit, Delilah settled onto the front porch alongside Virginia.

She felt a sudden tug to be closer to the woman who had taken her in, to feel her presence as though it was part of her own being. She longed for the serenity and simplicity that age seemed to bring and looked to Virginia as a kind of distant beacon guiding her through tumultuous terrain.

In the way the lost latch onto a savior—seeing more, perhaps, than what is there, but finding what they need—Delilah clung to the image of Virginia as a pillar among ruins.

She spent most of her young life convincing herself that, having no guidance, no role models, no one to whom she could look for inspiration, she therefore had no need of one. But now Virginia, simply by her existence, had drawn attention to a void within Delilah, and she yearned to have it filled.

Virginia left the outside light off to keep the moths away and to let the cool, easy darkness settle in around her. She belonged there, in the evening, on the porch, in this world. "Something on your mind?" she asked the girl while rocking serenely back and forth, the light from the moon casting faint shadows across her face.

Crickets rang through the still, night air, the rocker creaked occasionally on the porch floor, and they were all sounds of comfort and belonging.

Delilah pulled her feet up beneath her in the wicker chair and twirled the frayed ends of her jean shorts around her index finger. Was there something on her mind? Besides everything? "Have you always lived here, Virginia?"

"Oh, no. Actually did most of my growing up in Maine along the seashore. It was a wonderful childhood of playing in the rolling surf, collecting shells—I always smelled of salt and sun."

"I've never seen the ocean. I mean, I've never been there."

Virginia pursed her lips. "Never been to the ocean? Well. That's a tragedy."

"I imagine it's beautiful."

Virginia smiled. "Oh, yes. But so much more, too. To stand on a jetty so that land is completely behind you and all you see is the vast, curving expanse of the ocean with the breeze tousling your hair and the sound of the waves smashing against the beach—it's transcendent."

Delilah's gaze unfocused as she listened, Virginia's voice becoming lilting and musical, and Delilah could feel a sad wistfulness welling up inside her. Longing. She entwined her fingers and pressed her hands hard into her lap until she felt the clench in her stomach subside.

"But," Virginia continued, "when I was sixteen my father died and my mother and I moved in here with my aunt."

"Was it hard?"

"Moving? No, not really. I had never been *anywhere* so I was thrilled to be leaving our little neck of the woods. Even if it was just to come to another one. Why do you ask?"

"No reason. Just curious."

"Hmm." Virginia knew Delilah's questions were never simple, never idle. This child was starving for information. "Well, what else can I tell you?" A bat swooped past the porch eave and vanished into the surrounding shadows.

Delilah shrugged and pulled a thread from the hem of her shorts, rolled it into a ball between her thumb and forefinger and flicked it over the porch railing.

"Well, as long as you got me in the mood for talking, maybe I'll share something with you." Virginia paused until Delilah looked up at her. "Do you believe in ghosts?"

"I think just about anything is possible." Although when she was alone, at night, fighting sleep, Delilah prayed that when the time came it was truly the end. There had to be an end.

Virginia's eyes lit up. "That's my girl! You are a jewel, Delilah." She reached forward and patted Delilah on the hand. "Well—for the past several months I have had regular visits from Carl."

Delilah remained silent. She supposed it was possible, knew there were things beyond our comprehension, but she also knew that Virginia was tired and lonely.

"You don't believe me."

Delilah took a breath and smiled. "Actually, I do. If you say it's true, then I believe you."

"Hah! I knew you would. I knew you were the one to share it with! The first time I felt the soft brush of Carl's fingers across my cheek — well — I wanted to run screaming. I thought I surely must have, finally, lost my mind. But now, after a time of having it happen sort of regularly, I look forward to feeling him nearby."

"You haven't told anyone else?" Delilah suddenly felt tremendously privileged.

"And have them call me a crazy old bat? No thanks!"

"Amos wouldn't do that."

Virginia paused. "No. No, Amos wouldn't."

A sudden breeze blew then, both warm and chilled at the same time, and as the two eddies twined around one another they brushed bare legs and arms and necks.

Delilah wrinkled her nose. "What is that? It smells like—like..."

"Gasoline." Virginia drew her sweater a little tighter around herself and smiled, her eyes glassy with tears. "That's him Delilah. That's Carl." Then she laughed—not like a mature woman on the back one-quarter of her life, but like the young girl she must have been when she and Carl first met.

And maybe it was just the angle of the moonlight, or the way the breeze blew her hair across her forehead, but for a moment it appeared the delicate lines of age and sorrow lifted, revealing the countenance of that same young girl of the laughter. Suddenly Delilah saw Virginia in another world—holding hands with Carl, her lips cherry red and leaving imprints on coffee cups and soda glasses. She heard big band music, high heels on wooden dance floors, and the laughter of stolen kisses.

"Virginia, can I ask you a question?" Delilah spoke softly, not wanting to dispel the tenuous sense of magic in the air.

"You just did." Virginia smiled.

Delilah laughed. It's something she, herself, would have said. "Why didn't you have any children?"

Virginia's smile shifted, changing into a poignant, bittersweet gesture of remembrance. "I did. A little girl. But she was stillborn. We tried again, Carl and I, but it turned out I couldn't have any more."

"Oh. God. I'm sorry." She hurt for Virginia, who would have made an enviable mother. And in a world full of parents less deserving, less caring, less capable, it seemed horribly unfair. She would have loved to have been Virginia's daughter. How different her life might have been.

Virginia reached for Delilah's hand. "Oh, sweetheart, that's okay. It's long in the past. I always figured it was because I was meant to give my love elsewhere." She waited for Delilah to meet her gaze. "You, for instance."

Then the breeze died down, Virginia took a long, deep breath, and she was as she had been—beautiful, aging, alone, and still so very much in love.

Delilah clenched her jaw and drew a deep, steadying breath. It didn't matter, however, because one stray tear managed to break free, rolling down her cheek faster than she could catch it and wipe it away. She thought to say, "Thank you", or "I love you too," but nothing would cooperate—heart, mouth, brain, all flailing helplessly against one another, so she simply kissed Virginia gently on the cheek and went inside.

Virginia closed her eyes, one hand poised over her heart.

Yes, she missed Carl. They were worlds apart in a way she never thought they would be. She'd always had an admittedly childish notion that they would go together when the time came, holding hands, so that neither would be left behind.

Nevertheless, she had found a certain amount of peace as of late. She knew it would not be long before they would be together again. Everything moved in cycles. Everything.

And a cycle always came back around to its beginning.

In the woods off Main Street, Harold paced the length of his front porch in the dim glow of light spilling out from the living room. The itch in his brain was back, deeper this time and more persistent. He held a finger to the spot just above and behind his ear, massaging in tiny circles as though it would reach through skin and bone to the soft tissue beneath.

And if the itch wasn't enough, he didn't feel very well. Something in his stomach. Like it was empty, but heavy, tight, scrunched up like a balled fist, the tightness stretching up into the middle of his chest. And he couldn't get Delilah out of his mind. Maybe something of Delilah had gotten inside his head, inside his stomach, spreading like the frost on the window pane when he sat and watched if for hours in the winter. Maybe something of her had gotten in there and wouldn't leave until... until...

Out of the uneasiness, the emptiness in his gut, came fear. A cold, solitary fear that made him want to reach out and retreat and the same time. The contradictory needs worked against one another until he couldn't move at all, save for mesmerizing rocking from left to right. Left to right. Rocking.

Delilah. He thought.

Delilah had discovered that in small towns like Macaenas, when the last people turned out their lights for the night, it seemed they had hit the switch for the whole world. No blackness fell denser than that of remote country nights. No darkness more complete and consuming.

Nightlife was reserved for things wild. Bats tumbled through shadows, owls perched stonily on limbs, their eyes incandescent in the moonlight, housecats recalled their ancestry and stalked the fields for moles and mice; but the streets remained empty of things human, providing a glimpse into the simple wildness of a world without people.

Save for Delilah, who stole out of the house after all others were firmly embedded in dreams and delirium, and wandered—another restless spirit—Ophelia-like down empty roadways and through tangled woods and fields.

There was never any destination, and sometimes the nightly strolls meant nothing more than a few yards down the road to simply stand—alone, safe, free.

She would stand perfectly still, an ethereal figure, hearing nothing more than her own breath mixing with a gentle wind. Were someone to pass by, he might have even caught her humming softly to herself—a made-up tune or forgotten memory crooned to dusty night-shadows.

Sleeping was something Delilah did little of. The moment her eyes were closed she felt trapped, as though a gate had shut, locking her deep inside herself. The only way sleep would ever win out was through persistence; exhaustion was necessary before she would concede.

And it was just that—concession. In the same manner as defeat.

Sleep left her exposed.

So she had the nights of Macaenas to herself to pad silently down winding roads, or lie in the fields dizzying herself with the stars. Or sometimes she walked past Amos' house and watched his shadow pace by the window in the blue light of the television. Or she'd sit on the grass at the edge of the woods across the street and wonder what kind of love would leave such an ache behind. What must it be like to feel that passionately about another human being? She could not imagine. Watching Amos was like watching an alien creature— immensely fascinating, but ultimately incomprehensible. She knew he had possessed something of which she had no knowledge.

This night, however, as she lay on her back near the pond, the grass damp with dew, a frightening memory struck her, one so terrifying that she sat straight up, clumps of grass gripped inside her clenched fists.

Before she had gotten on the bus that finally landed her here, back when her life was all fear and no love, she slept for a week with a piece of paper under her pillow, hoping it would bring her pleasant dreams of an unknown future. On that paper she had written: Bus #89—Holm? Brooks Hill? Macaenas?? Sharontown?

She forgot about it when she left—alone, in the dark. It remained behind, waiting—waiting for, perhaps, a rage to send those pillows tossed to the floor, leaving it exposed. Waiting.

Had he found it? Oh god, did he know?

When Amos first opened his eyes in the morning his initial reaction was always immense disappointment.

If he were able, he would fill his days with long, continuous stretches of uninterrupted slumber. Only then did the weight of his life's unexplainable nature leave his shoulders. Only then did he feel a sense of freedom from all things earthly, and therefore uncontrollable.

At night he dreamed as though he'd traveled back in time.

Rarely were the dreams of crucial events, but rather seemingly inconsequential moments like Ellen's first day coming "home" to his house after work. She had just moved in with him, and as the Toyota pulled in the drive from Sinclair Elementary at four o'clock, he stood on the front porch like a boy, hands casually in pockets, leaning against the post, an immense, cockeyed grin on his face as she stepped out of the car.

128

"What the hell are you smiling at, you lunatic?" She grabbed some books from the car's backseat, aware of him eyeing the shape of her backside.

"At my woman coming home to me." He tried in vain to control the sloppy grin that threatened to leap clear off his face into the sunshine.

"'Your woman,' huh?" She stood beside the car, books held to her chest, one hip cocked to one side and the sun lighting her from behind like a blissful apparition.

"Good God, you're beautiful," he said.

Ellen stood perfectly still, her knuckles clenching the bookbindings as the tears welled to overflowing even before the sound of his voice made it all the way to her heart.

Then that image bled into others, some real, some imagined—doing the crossword puzzle in bed (real), picnics in fields of cartoon wildflowers, their children laughing in the distance (imagined)—which melted into others, on and on throughout the night, an endless line of perfect, precious images like pearls on a string.

Dreams.

So his mornings consisted of long moments lying in bed, reluctant to let go those last strains of sleep and dreams, only slowly allowing the sharp light of cognizance to mercilessly flood his brain.

That moment—where he took the jagged step back into waking reality—was unfailingly painful, as it carried the realization that all those images of Ellen were no more than ghosts in his mind, no more solid than the breath he struggled to take.

"Amos! Wake up! Amos!" This morning Delilah calling to him from the foot of the porch stairs roused him from the comfort of sleep.

Dragging himself from bed he leaned close to the screen, "What the hell are you doing? I was asleep! It's my day off, for Chrissake!"

"Precisely!" she called back. "Come see! Amos, please, come see!"

"No! Jesus, Delilah! It's too early!" The dreams had been particularly vivid and he longed to return to them, to dissolve into their soft embrace no matter how false the contact.

"Please! Amos, you have to see!"

It was clear she would not move until he relented, that she would perch beneath his window indefinitely, like the blue jay that spent all day screeching in the elm tree, so he pulled on some clothes, put a baseball hat over his sleep-mashed hair, and begrudgingly stomped downstairs to meet the charming, occasionally aggravating Delilah in his front yard.

But then he suddenly remembered what he'd done to her, the rage he'd thrown at her and a wash of shame stopped him on the porch and forced him to look at her.

She was already back through the front gate when he came through the door. Unable to stand still, like a child at Christmas, she bounced on her toes and turned in circles, waving for him to hurry and follow. She was like a sparrow, flitting from branch to fencepost to grass and back again. No remnant of his verbal attack on her was evident.

For a moment they regarded each other with bemused curiosity, then Amos took a breath to apologize, to plead stupidity, insanity, anything so that she wouldn't hold it against him, but before he could utter a word Delilah broke into a contagious, Cheshire Cat grin and like a playful foal, she turned tail and bolted. Amos, as though caught in her wake, found himself falling quickly into step behind her, his body instantly crying out in protest. He could not recall the last time he ran.

"What the hell time is it, Delilah?" He wheezed between gasping breaths. "I don't even know!"

"I don't know, Amos! What difference does it make?"

"Delilah!" He nearly stopped, let her go on. He ached for the comfort of home and bed—and dreams—but running ahead of him, she was all light and sweetness and full of something he honestly wished he could possess himself. Though he didn't know its name.

She led him across Main Street to Carver's Park and over to the pond where, finally, mercifully, she stopped, her back to him, but her body tense and humming, like a struck piano wire.

"Delilah..." he panted hard, out of breath, bending to brace his hands against his thighs and calm his racing heart, straining lungs. The sun fell across his back, warming tense muscles, and he focused on its comfort.

Then he saw them. Drifting serenely across the surface of the pond as he quietly stepped up beside her.

"They mate for life, you know." She whispered, her voice full of awe and quiet wonder.

The swans waltzed gracefully together, their long, question-mark necks arching toward one another until their bills touched, forming a perfect heart shape. They intertwined a moment before pulling away and beginning again in a flawless *pas-de-deux.*

"Well I'll be damned," Amos whispered, "I don't ever remember seeing swans here before. In fact, I've never seen them in the wild."

"They're so tender with each other." Delilah's voice seemed to come from a great distance away as though puzzling over some confusion. "So loving."

Amos turned away. He felt a sudden jab in his chest as though fingernails had dug into the soft, tender flesh of his heart. His eyes burned, and his throat tightened, sucking all the air from his struggling lungs. He didn't want this—not now. Not ever. These feelings were supposed to be gone. He was suffocating.

But a soft touch on his shoulder cooled the fire and brought him back from the nightmare.

He turned to Delilah, the swans visible over her shoulder, and found he had no words to speak. With all that screamed within him, he was as silent as the swans.

"That's how much you love her, isn't it? I knew it the minute I saw them here."

Speechless, Amos watched the swans glide behind her, saw how they seemed to need to touch one another, to be near one another, how they appeared to regard each other with such reverent respect and—love?

Or perhaps he simply projected that upon them in his need to experience it himself.

Is this it? Is the whole rest of his life doomed to dwell in the shadows of what could have been? Why bother? Why care?

"The winter before they found the cancer," Amos began, before he even realized he had anything to say, "Ellen bought us both ice skates for Christmas. I had never been on skates in my life, but the winter had come fast and cold and the pond froze solid—Ellen wanted to go and I could refuse her nothing.

"I was disastrous. A lumbering bear." He laughed, a short, explosive sound, as the memory solidified, blocking out the swans and the park and the sunshine until it was all he could see. Just cold and ice and Ellen. "But Ellen—well—as always, she put me in awe. I gave up, just sat on the rocks and played spectator." He paused, the memory shifting, his eyes dimming. "As I watched her laughing, spinning, occasionally falling down with all the bravado and enthusiasm of a child, I was overcome by the thought of losing her. I don't know why, but as she skated she actually appeared to be slipping away from me, and this—hallucination— became so vivid that I leapt to my feet and called to her." The memory had taken over, and his hands reached out as if Ellen were there. "She came to me, and I grabbed her so fiercely that I frightened her. I frightened myself.

"The following spring she was diagnosed."

He paused, suddenly aware of his own voice, startled by it. Embarrassed by it. Then he turned toward Delilah, but as he was lost in his own past, she had quietly slipped away, leaving him alone with the morning, the swans, and one of Virginia's magic apple muffins cradled in his cupped hands.

He couldn't breathe.

Unable to stand still, nowhere to go, Amos wandered down Main street until he found himself turning down the drive to Harold's house. He didn't know why, perhaps it was simply he knew he could find silent company there. A place to be alone, but not alone.

"Amos!" An unexpected voice greeted him and looking up he saw Virginia sitting on a kitchen chair on the porch, Harold on the steps eating a muffin.

"Virginia! Well, hello!" He ambled up the porch steps and gingerly lowered himself onto another, less sturdy chair.

"How are you?" She did not look at him when she asked.

Amos felt like a child, insecure, uncertain, full of mistakes and misunderstandings. "I'm fine. And apparently Delilah's fine." He touched her arm to get her attention. "I'm sorry," he said when she looked up.

"You don't owe me an apology."

"I think I do."

"Well, you don't, but if it makes you feel better..." She smiled at him and looked away, signalling that was the end of the matter.

Amos shook his head and laughed. He was lucky to have people like Virginia. "Making a delivery?" He gestured to Harold.

"Yeah. It's been a little while since I've been out here and I was feeling guilty." She fanned herself with a folded sheet of paper.

"Hm. I know that feeling. It's so hard. I know he likes to be alone, but, well, nobody should be alone all of the time."

"Good advice." She eyed him playfully.

"Are you implying that I spend too much time alone?"

"I'm not implying anything. You can take it any way you want." She laughed and looked off into the woods.

"Yeah. You aren't implying anything. I've known you too long, Virginia. Besides, with Delilah around I'd be *lucky* to get a little solitude."

Virginia laughed. "Yup. She's a kicker, all right."

"That's one word for her." Amos smiled now.

Virginia waved him away. "Oh, please. You love every minute of her."

Amos sighed, still smiling. "I suppose I do. To be honest, I feel a little odd about that sometimes."

"What?"

"I don't know. The fact that I feel -- something for her."

"You mean you love her."

Amos did not respond right away. "I guess." He could feel a flush rise in his face although he couldn't explain why.

"Amos -- there are lots of different kinds of love. No offense, but you're too old not to know that."

Amos laughed. "Of course I know that. I don't know what it is."

"You're not telling me you feel *romantic* love for her, are you?" There was no shock in Virginia's voice, in fact, she sounded amused.

"No! Jesus, Virginia!"

"Oh please. It's not like that's out of the question, like it's never happened before."

"Maybe so, but it's not the case here. I guess – I guess it's just that whatever 'kind' of love it is, it's so intense. I mean, it's like she demands that if you care for her, you do it with all your heart and soul. And yet, in actuality, she demands nothing. Nothing at all."

"That's why she makes us feel that way." Virginia reached over and patted Amos on the hand like he was no more than thirteen. "You go ahead and love her, Amos. It's good for you. It's good for all of us to feel that."

Below them on the steps, Harold had turned toward them, rocking back and forth and watching them. When they both noticed, he pulled his gaze away, redirecting it toward his sneakers. "Delilah..." he said softly.

Amos shook his head. "He sure has latched onto something about her. I mean, I don't think he's actually come face to face with her, but somewhere along the line he picked up her name."

"He's got a lot more going on in there than people give him credit for. That's what I think."

"'A friend is a person with whom I may be sincere. Before him, I may think aloud.' Ralph Waldo Emerson." Harold spoke abruptly and just as curtly fell silent.

His meaning could have been empty, but so could it be full of any number of cryptic messages. Virginia and

Amos could only erupt with wondrous, surrendering laughter.

"Oh, Harold!" Virginia clapped her hands together. "You are a treasure! And I do love you."

Harold remained focused on his sneakers, but behind the muffin held cupped to his mouth, he smiled.

Morning slipped to afternoon, and upon returning to his house Amos found Delilah sitting on his front steps.

"Well, hello there." He spoke as he walked through the gate.

"Do you believe in God?" she asked him.

He laughed and rubbed his eyes. "You have an odd way of starting conversations, Delilah."

She smiled as he approached and settled on the step beside her. "Do you?"

"No, I don't. Although I sometimes think my life would be easier if I did. Why?"

"Really? Why?"

He noted her avoidance of his question, but moved beyond it. It was nothing new. "Because then I'd have someone to blame. An easy reason for the unpleasantness of life. That's the only reason I can see why anyone believes. Instead, I demand complicated answers to my complex questions. Simply passing it all off to the fickle mind of an unknowable supreme being is insulting and only seeks to placate me rather than answer me. I think believing in God is something weak people do so that they don't have to take responsibility and don't have to ask hard questions that might lead to a difficult truth."

She stared at him with a half smile.

"You asked," he said.

"Yes I did. What truth?"

Amos thought a moment, unsure what would happen if he spoke the words aloud. Would he damn them all? Or set them free? "That we are alone."

"Hm." Delilah rested her chin on her hand.

"What?"

"Nothing. I'm thinking. Deciding if I agree with you."

"Ah." He swatted away a fly that had landed on his hand.

"Don't you want to know?" Delilah smiled.

"I thought you were still thinking."

"I'm finished."

"Oh. Well, then, by all means, let's hear it."

"I think..." she paused, as though drawing together a tome of thoughts, funneling them down into one, perfunctory spark of wisdom. "You think too much."

Amos sat staring, trying to discern whether she was serious or joking. Her tone suggested the former, but her impish smile opposed that. "Really?" was all he finally mustered.

"Yup. While I'm all for some profound, internal deep-sea diving, sometimes you just need to know what you *feel*. What do you *feel*, Amos?"

The question reduced him to a wide-eyed dumbfounded child. She might as well have asked how many stars were in the sky. "I don't know."

"Well," Delilah concluded, "therein lies your problem." She smiled, full of that unknown thing Delilah possessed that sometimes caused her to glow.

"I didn't know I had a problem." He cocked an eyebrow at her.

Delilah stood, the sun a copper halo about her head, and touched his cheek with the back of her hand in a gesture that was both maternal and romantic. Amos forgot how to breathe. Then she turned to leave, paused, and turned back to him, laying her hand over his heart and looking him squarely in the eye. Amos thought if he didn't get a breath soon, surely he would pass out.

"You are a good man, Amos." She said, and stepped off his porch, and toward the front gate

Amos watched her, his breath returning to normal with each step she took away from him.

"Delilah!" he suddenly called out, needing, finally to say it, to be sure she knew.

"I know, Amos," she said, paused on the other side of his fence. "It's okay."

It should have made him feel better, but somehow it didn't. Somehow, it almost made him feel worse.

Afternoon faded to dusk, waited for darkness.

Something had grabbed hold of Amos and refused to let go.

He stood in his backyard as though he didn't recognize it, arms stiffly at his sides, head slightly upturned, his eyes flicking from leaf to flower to bird to leaf, unable to identify or settle on any one thing. He could see the world spinning.

He could not gain control over his heart, which had taken to beating frenetically all the time, leaving him constantly winded.

Through the whirling fog in his mind he kept thinking of Delilah. It was her. She had unleashed this—thing—that now consumed him, and although it flooded him with warm memories of Ellen, it also ignited agonizing longings that he had managed to keep caged for so long.

Time was supposed to heal all wounds, but time had passed and nothing had changed.

He was alone.

Across the yard, Delilah stood in her bedroom window, watching Amos standing as though he hoped to grow roots. She saw something familiar in his aloneness. Something profound and endless and necessary.

She wished she could tell him that.

She wished he knew.

Overhead a red-tailed hawk let out its trumpeting screech as it spun lazy circles above the trees, and two pairs of eyes tilted upward, envious of its freedom from the heavy pull of a very tired earth.

Jack Gruffen looked in the mirror over the dresser of his highway motel room and rubbed his hands over his beard stubble. Bloodshot eyes stared back at him, red spider-veins running tracks through the whites like roads on a map. For every mile, another vein.

He could no longer recall just how far he'd come, miles disappearing behind him in a blur of pavement and distraction, and he was still unsure of exactly where he was headed. Although he had a pretty good idea.

"Shit. You're a goddamn mess, Gruffen," he thought as he fingered a disposable razor on the dresser beside his wallet, car keys, and a handful of crumpled up papers and receipts. He should shave, get presentable, and get back on the road, but at the moment his head ached and the heat outside made him nauseous, and the Dart reeked of warm beer and old cigarettes, so he lay back on the bed in his air-conditioned room and slept.

Everything would still be there when he woke. Everything had to be somewhere.

In the early morning hours, Delilah lay in bed listening to the sounds of Virginia's rising -- the faint, brief creak of her bedroom door, a few seconds of silence as she made her way to the stairs across the runner splashed with golden sunflowers, then the soft plunk of her footfalls and the occasional groan of stair as she descended to the first floor, all the while a distant humming wafting around her, sometimes a tune heavy and sad, other times light and skipping.

She would follow the sound until it faded at the foot of the stairs when Virginia turned toward the kitchen, then she would roll over on her bed to the window and lean her head on the sill, the sound re-emerging from the kitchen window below. The tune sometimes grew words and was joined by the easy sounds of running water, dishes pinging together, and eventually the sweet, rich aroma of Virginia's apple muffins and coffee.

Every morning she began her day to this kind of real-life symphony, and always it brought a light, brief string of pearly tears that ran off the back of her hand as her chin rested on the windowsill. It filled the house with a kind of tangible normalcy she had always longed for. It hung in the air like cotton candy, wispy and sweet, but that very sweetness also brought a melancholy that crawled around inside her like a cat circling a place to sleep, and only through a wash of tears could she keep it from settling in for good.

It had taken her and Virginia no more than the blink of an eye to forge a fierce and loving bond that resembled that of the closest families, to weave a relationship that belied its brief history and spoke volumes of their deep and kindred souls.

That connection had snuck up on Delilah. She hadn't felt she'd been looking for one, not with anything or anyone.

Her life, at the time, was fragmented and about independence. She didn't know that independence and intimacy were not mutually exclusive.

In a world where the same hand that soothes can harm and the same eyes that comfort can lie, where words often mean the opposite and the sound of your own voice can bring startling tears, standing on one's own meant standing a great distance away.

But Virginia's tender ways and gentle heart touched a soft, forgotten place in Delilah. It made her think of fresh laundry hanging in the sun, and teddy bears, and warm, rescuing hugs. Things she'd once had, things she'd never had, things she'd always dreamed of.

Virginia sat in the kitchen with her first coffee of the day, staring out the window and thinking about her life since Delilah had arrived. She had felt so much of her heart wither when Carl died that she thought it would never be full again. She had accepted the fact that sounds came duller, colors looked muted, and the air entered her lungs carrying wiry bristles that scraped her insides.

Until Delilah.

Delilah's quiet defiance and masked frailty drew Virginia out of her own, bleak pain in an effort to reach out to a young woman alone. To look at Delilah was to view such infinite complexities enmeshed with such basic simplicities that one tended to wonder if she was of this earth at all. Yet the ridge of scars on her wrist and the infinitesimal flashes of sad uncertainty in her eyes confirmed that she was, indeed, of the same world as everyone else.

"No one need feel alone in this world, child. There is always *someone* who cares." Virginia had said to her the very first day Delilah showed up on her front porch, dripping wet, and in need of something the outside world had failed to provide her.

It was advice Virginia needed to remind herself of every once in a while.

Before breakfast, as she did every morning, Delilah climbed out one of the attic dormers and sat on the slope of the roof. It was the one thing she did that she knew unsettled Virginia, and while Delilah accepted much of Virginia's advice and adjusted for many of Virginia's concerns, she remained stubborn about the roof. How could she explain that it had always been one place where no one could reach her? Where only the surest footed (and bravest of heart) could find her. She had considered on more than one occasion just saying the words, just the way she heard them in her head. But they seemed to vanish every time she took a breath to speak them.

Delilah's habit unsettled Amos as well. He saw her there often in early evenings or weekend mornings, and although he initially had the urge to call to her, to ask her what the hell she was doing, he never had, and now he didn't care to. There was something about her as she sat there. Something in the way she held her body so motionless as she stared off toward the horizon as though the strength of her stare held that thin line between earth and sky in place.

It so compelled him that one night (he did not have the courage to venture out in the openness of daylight) he made his way to his own roof to find out what Delilah saw from her perch. But one false step and a heart-wrenching tumble to the rain gutters quickly snuffed his curiosity and reminded him he was far to old to possess the strange and dramatic longings of youth. Instead he settled for a surreptitious study of her as he took his walks. And maybe, one day, he'd go ahead and ask. Not today though. Today he stood beneath the dappled shade of a beech tree and watched her motionless figure—part Buddha, part stunt person, part lonely little girl. Sometimes the urge to swallow her in his arms and hold her safe overwhelmed him. But was that urge meant to comfort her, or himself?

"Delilah!" Virginia stuck her head out the kitchen window and called up to her. "Breakfast is on!" As she withdrew she noticed Amos paused in the street. "Amos! Good morning!"

"Good morning, Virginia."

"Since you're here, why don't you join us?"

Amos hesitated, knowing he'd been caught spying, but when Delilah met his eyes as she climbed back in and waved to him, smiling, he agreed. That infectious smile; he could deny it nothing.

Virginia had always been a wonderful cook from the old school. She still made breakfast as though cooking for a houseful, with fresh fruit and eggs, homemade muffins and her coffee had a touch of cinnamon.

In fact, the entire house always radiated a soft warmth that bid welcome to anyone who crossed the threshold. It held no bias, no judgments; if you walked through the door you were home, whether for five minutes, five hours, or five years.

"I'm glad I caught you walking by this morning, Amos." Virginia poured the coffee into blue china cups, then sat at the table as Amos scanned the amazing spread of food. He rubbed his hands together.

"So am I. I'm lucky if I manage to make myself a bowl of cornflakes in the morning." He smiled at her. He'd been trying hard to move past the gremlins that wove dark patterns in his mind and Virginia always proved a positive ally in that.

145

She waved her hand, "Cornflakes! That's not breakfast! That's squirrel food for chrissake!" She took the sugar and sifted three, small spoonfuls into her cup. The spoon clinked against the china like a tiny, distant chime.

Delilah appeared from upstairs and joined them, taking a large gulp of fresh orange juice before she got all the way into her chair. As she held the glass to her mouth Amos noticed the scar on her wrist again -- a dark, raised line along the center of her small arm. This time it was clearly visible, targeting him with its once-felt pain.

There are times when moments elongate to the point of resembling entire days -- it happened when they got the news of Ellen's cancer -- and it happened now, as the sight of the scar snared his attention. He became trapped by its angry sadness, uncomfortably caught by the curiosity it demanded, and yet he stared until Delilah finally drained the glass and set it on the table, thus removing the scar from view.

In retrospect Amos recalled Delilah standing with her hands in her pockets, behind her back, folded across her chest, or sitting with them pressed together between her knees. Hindsight provided a clarity showing those poses to be so practiced, so rehearsed, that to the casual observer they appeared natural, unremarkable, real. Perhaps she'd performed them for so long they had become just that, even to her.

"God, I'm starving this morning." Delilah said.

"Oh, I left the skim milk in the fridge. Would you mind grabbing that for us?" Virginia asked.

146

"Sure." Delilah rose from the table and disappeared through the swinging door to the kitchen.

Virginia reached over and touched Amos' arm, coaxing him out of his introspection, her voice hushed in secrecy. "She's never spoken of them. Those scars. She doesn't really hide them, but she doesn't talk about them."

Amos shook his head in silent understanding. He wanted to say more, to talk it out, and try to understand, but Delilah returned with the milk.

When Amos left Virginia's (after she refused to let him help her clean up) he walked to the pond. Seeing the scar on Delilah's wrist left him haunted and sad and full of questions. What could so torment a young, vibrant, forgiving girl like Delilah that she would resort to suicide? Would witnessing the act in a parent encourage or deter you? He could not imagine the desperation you'd have to feel -- the extreme and total hopelessness required -- to propel yourself to such a dark and final act.

Even in his worst moments -- the isolation of his childhood, the loss of his parents, and of course, the death of Ellen—he never felt himself fall into that suffocating abyss.

Or, perhaps he had. Perhaps that was the growing void he'd begun to feel surrounding him, and yet it was not powerful enough to drive him toward that everlasting decision. It took a certain amount of courage, he thought, to make a choice which, if successful, was irreversible.

His view of Delilah altered.

He couldn't quite put his finger on precisely *how*, it felt like an odd mix of admiration, sorrow, and pride. One would think pity would have found its way in there as well, but it didn't.

There was nothing pitiful about Delilah. No matter what life had thrown her thus far, she elicited no pity. And to possess those scars, Amos thought, she must have been thrown an awful lot.

He lay back into the prickly grass, his hands folded behind his head, distantly aware of the sounds of the mysterious swans splashing in the pond, and watched incoming clouds wash over the sun.

The earth spun at approximately 25,000 miles per hour and he wondered for a moment if the reason he couldn't see the sky whisking by was simply because it was all the same shade of blue. Flat, pale hazy blue.

25,000 miles per hour! And we feel nothing because we, too, are traveling at that speed. Lying perfectly still on a small patch of summer-browned grass, a ball of gnats swirling overhead, he traveled at 25,000 miles per hour and couldn't feel a thing.

Not a thing.

Suddenly the humidity increased sharply and along with it came a strong gust of wind. A storm was coming. The wind licked sharply at leaves, flipping them up to reveal silver undersides, then dying down a moment before building strength again, sending the arms of the willow trees sweeping back and forth across the pond like the long hems of women's skirts and making the swans restless as it blew ripples across the surface of the water.

By the time Amos realized how fast the front was moving in, it was too late. The rain hit as he crossed Main Street onto Haven Lane as though the sky's back had suddenly broken, all it had been carrying crashing down at once.

The sky instantly darkened from the flat color of a dull nickel to deep, charcoal grey, split by arcing, angry arms of lightning that cut the air between earth and sky, while explosions of thunder rattled his breastbone as though trying to shake loose his ribs.

"Holy Jesus!" Amos hollered into the unyielding rain, unable, at first, to recall the last time he'd seen a storm like this one.

By the time he reached his porch, the edges of the road had turned to small, running streams. Basements would flood. The pond would overflow, creating a swamp all the way to the gazebo. Now he remembered. The last time.

He was twelve years old. A storm like this trapped him in the gazebo in the park. He'd been studying a praying mantis when the storm rolled in fast with no warning, leaving him huddled on the floor of the insubstantial shelter, awed and terrified until a small break came in the downpour. Ready to make a run for it he jumped off the gazebo and sank nearly shin-deep into swampy mud and water.

Now, finally shutting the door behind him he stood a moment, dripping, listening to harsh sheets of rain pelt the windows and the wind buffet the sides of the house, snatching at wooden shingles.

This storm wanted in.

Then, behind the rumble and whistling wind he heard the phone ringing.

"What the..." Not wanting to traipse through to the kitchen he made his way quickly upstairs to the bedroom, leaving a small trail of water in his wake. "Good Lord, Ellen, you cannot believe this storm." He spoke to her when he was anxious and he had never been one for storms. Ever since his childhood when the outlet in their living room shot bolts of electricity across the room during violent storms, he has seen them as evidence of a power and strength so much larger than the human race that we had no business parading around this planet like we owned it.

Meanwhile, in the time it took him to reach the landing, the phone stopped, mid-ring. *"Good,"* he thought. *"Who in their right mind would pick up a phone in the middle of all this?"*

In his bedroom he stripped down, wrung out his clothes in the adjoining bathroom tub and hung them over the shower curtain rod to drip dry.

He pulled on a dry t-shirt and a pair of jeans while in front of the window that faced Virginia's house, the view obstructed by the far-reaching arms of an old elm tree.

The next blinding flash of lightning and ferocious crack of thunder that followed snapped so viciously loud that for a moment Amos thought that he, himself, had been struck.

It left a ringing in his ears.

But then he heard the slow, harsh snapping and splintering of breaking wood and through the window he saw the elm tree split in half, one piece still rooted to the ground, the other falling toward Virginia's yard, crushing the small fence between it and his own.

That's when he saw her.

Unbelievably, Delilah sat perched outside that attic window, her grey t-shirt and shorts so plastered to her body they appeared painted on. She sat, leaning back against the slant of the roof, her face turned up toward the storm. She either smiled or grimaced, and she may have been crying but in the rain it was impossible to tell.

"What the..." he threw open the window and leaned out. "Delilah!" he shouted uselessly into the wind, ignoring the fact that his own dry t-shirt became immediately soaked through.

Retreating from the window he pulled on his work boots and ran back outside. The rain gave no sign of abating and impossibly, Amos thought, seemed to be growing stronger.

He ran around to the front of Virginia's house, threw open the gate, and went to the side of the house that faced his own. Another flash of lightning snapped in the sky and thunder shook the ground, already the lawn had grown spongy beneath him, the mud sucking greedily at his boots.

Above him sat Delilah. Still. Poised. Statue-like. A human gargoyle against the grey, raging skies. "Delilah! Dammit! What the hell are you doing?" He could smell the tree behind him smoldering; it made his nose itch. "DELILAH!"

Suddenly she moved. She blinked. She took a breath and turned her gaze to the ground below her. When she saw him she broke into an immense smile, her eyes wild as the storm. "Amos! Oh, can you hear that?"

Amos could barely hear *her*, and what he did hear he didn't understand. "Delilah! Get the hell down from there right now! Are you out of your mind?"

"Oh Amos!" Seemingly oblivious to both his furious demands and the storm, she lifted her arms to the sky like a child asking to be coddled just as a bolt of lightning cracked the power line off the peak of the roof, plunging the house into darkness. Amos could feel the ion charge tickling his skin and decided he'd had enough. Going to the shed in the backyard he grabbed an extension ladder and leaned it against the house. He didn't particularly relish the idea of standing atop a tall, metal object in the middle of a raging storm, but Delilah didn't seem to be moving on her own. He would have gone through the house to the attic windows, but if Virginia didn't already know about this he didn't want to panic her.

Nor did he care to make another attempt at roof-walking.

At the top of the ladder he reached his hand out to Delilah. "C'mon, Delilah, let's go. Not a great place to be just now."

She looked at him then and he could see, in spite of the rain, that it was not laughter twisting her expression. Her eyes were rimmed with harsh red, the vibrant, green irises muddied. "She must happy now, right?"

"Yeah. Sure. C'mon, Delilah. Let's go down." Amos started back down the ladder as Delilah moved toward him, all the fury and energy suddenly gone from her, left to the storm, making her nothing more than a girl soaked through to the bone.

Once on the ground Amos set the ladder alongside the house, put his arm around Delilah who now shivered uncontrollably, and led her inside. At the porch steps her legs gave way and Amos half carried her through the front door. For the first time since she arrived he feared for her. For her safety. Her sanity.

He sat her in the kitchen, found some candles to light, and went upstairs to get some towels from the bathroom. The Emmett home was as familiar as his own.

On his way he paused just once in the doorway to the kitchen and turned toward Delilah. She sat at the table, hands in her lap, body hunched toward the table, strands of wet hair falling forward over her face; she seemed to want to fold into herself, become smaller, compact, perhaps even disappear.

Amos swallowed hard and turned away. The girl radiated pain that he could feel in his own gut, and it unnerved him.

Travelling up the stairs, he fought to ignore the quick flashes through the windows and the grumbling in the sky. He mumbled under his breath to Ellen and focused on the task at hand.

Just before the bathroom stood Virginia's room, the door open, Virginia lying on her bed, legs crossed at the ankles, eyes gently closed.

"How the hell could she sleep through this storm?" Amos mused as he stepped passed the room.

Then he stopped. She couldn't. She feared storms more than he did. The sudden, fierce cracks of thunder made her jump and pace the house like a nervous cat, her hands wringing one over the other.

Backtracking he slipped quietly into her room, his heart beating in his temples. It smelled of lavender oil, furniture polish, and something else — something acrid and sweet hung barely noticeable beneath the other aromas and was vaguely familiar, although it didn't quite belong there.

Gasoline?

Virginia remained quiet and still, and Amos didn't need to cross the entire space between the door and the bed to know. For as violently as it raged outside, in that room it was numbingly still.

In the kitchen he covered Delilah with towels and made some coffee. Her tears had stopped, replaced by silent staring as she watched the steam rise from her coffee cup and the candle flames flicker on their stems.

"I called an ambulance, Delilah. They'll be here soon."

She nodded.

The rain had lessened some, but the sky remained dark and heavy. This storm would not go easily.

"She was good to me." Delilah spoke, lifting her tired gaze to Amos' as he leaned against the counter.

"As you were to her, Delilah. It's all she ever spoke of." He struggled to fight his own welling emotion. Oh, Virginia. "She was so alone before you got here. I can't tell you the difference you made for her."

"I know I haven't known her very long, but..." She didn't finish, her eyes dropping back to the table, an eruption of sobs choking in her throat.

Amos took the chair beside her, engulfing her small hand in his. They were cold, her hands, as though her blood could not reach them. He wanted to hold her, to enfold her in his arms and assure her it would all be all right, that the grief and the pain would pass, but he realized he wasn't sure he believed that himself. "It's not how long you know someone, Delilah. It's how deeply. You can know someone for a day and miss them like you've known them all your life."

$\mathcal{D}$elilah held the blade in her thirteen-year-old hand between her left thumb and forefinger. There was no time for thought, for contemplation, she could hear him calling for her downstairs. Oddly enough she cried no tears, simply took a deep breath and traced the blade along the length of her wrist. Then, switching hands, the right one already covered in blood, she repeated the movement on her left wrist. No pain.

Her father had reached the top of the stairs.

She held her wrists over the sink and stared at her reflection in the mirrored door of the medicine cabinet.

Her father knocked on the door. "Delilah?"

She did not answer, but for some reason she could not comprehend, she started to laugh. Instantly he threw the door open and froze at the sight -– his daughter's arms and hands spilling scarlet blood, her gaze locked to the mirror, laughing...

"Jesus Christ! What the hell are you doing?" Grabbing towels from behind the door he snatched Delilah away from the sink and wrapped the towels tightly around her wrists. "Goddamn it. What are you trying to do?" His voice came softly, fearfully, causing her to actually look into his eyes. But when he looked at her, his eyes fell dark. "What the fuck is wrong with you!" He shook her, knocking her head against the medicine cabinet so hard her vision wavered a moment. And when she began laughing again, beyond caring or feeling, all sense and reason gone, he backhanded her, cutting her cheek.

"Shit," he mumbled as he sat her on the edge of the bathtub, secured the towels, and picked her up to carry her out to the car.

The sun shone the day they buried Virginia, a brilliant, golden disk high in a pristine blue sky.

The ground was still soggy, mostly mud, summer gardens beaten down and drowned, but the sun defeated stubborn clouds to spread a little reassurance that things can, indeed, change.

But the message was slow in reaching everyone, sadness still clung too closely and rang too loudly, like the peal of church bells that filled the air.

The faces gathered at the cemetery resembled those from the Fourth of July, only with fewer smiles, and no joy. Celebration and mourning. Both brought the town together (and sold hats as well, apparently, as not one woman present stood without one). Several yards away from the gravesite Harold sat alone on a stone bench hunched over a book, surreptitiously keeping watch. No one noticed. No one's tears fell upon his shoulder, no one's arms encircled his willowy body sending heat and strength and kinship. Only the sun came to warm him, only the stone on which he sat supported him; his persistent rocking quietly soothed him. No one noticed. Except Delilah, who -- in spite of Amos' insistence that she belonged as much as any of them, moreso even -- also chose to remain separate from the rest. She stood a short distance away, wrapped in Virginia's borrowed scarf, eyes hidden beneath dark glasses, her shadow falling long and thin across the muddied grass, while long-time friends gathered close by and close together to say their final farewells. She glanced briefly at Harold, simply noting his existence, not thinking much further on it than the acknowledgment of another familiar face. Vaguely familiar. And alone. She might have pondered further on it had she not been full of thoughts of death; how those she loved the most seemed to always suddenly leave her. It made it difficult not to feel there was a direct correlation between the two, as though her love carried some sort of deadly virus. Or, did she simply love too fiercely? Did the force of it leave no room for anything else, even life itself?

Amos was asked to say a few words, and as he spoke of Virginia and her life in this world, he spoke over the heads of those encircling the grave toward Delilah. She stood too far away to hear the actual words, but he felt certain she would hear the meaning. She must know that Virginia left this world truly happy and loved, and that she had everything to do with that.

158

When the service was finished, clasped circles broken and the first handful of dirt thrown on the coffin, Amos looked up to where Delilah stood, but she was gone. Just an empty patch of sun.

As always, the ghost among them.

But he didn't know she hadn't gone far.

Just over a small hill she had found Harold watching a small, dusty-brown rabbit nibbling a patch of clover. She kept her distance, understanding him to be as private a person as she. Wariness wafted around his head like faint puffs of smoke.

When she took another step, drawn to him, both Harold and the rabbit stiffened, Harold's head turning just a fraction toward the sound, although not enough for her to see his face. Nevertheless he radiated fragileness, as timid and skittish as the rabbit he spied upon. At the same time, an unmistakable force hung between them, one that pulled each toward the other in some unspoken recognition.

But Harold would never acknowledge that. Risks were too high, uncertainty to potent.

But Delilah would. "Hi," she said. "I saw you at the funeral, by yourself. I just wanted to see if you were okay."

Harold bit the side of his cheek and glanced quickly toward her and away again.

"Did you know Virginia well?" The effort was as much for herself as for him, perhaps moreso, in that she began to feel a sense of panic in her aloneness. Where before her solitude was of her own choosing, this— Virginia's absence—had been forced upon her.

Harold remained silent for a moment, almost holding his breath, his heart pounding within his chest. When he spoke it was barely a sound, but nevertheless it startled the rabbit into scampering into the bushes. "'I'm Nobody. Who are you?'" He paused, regaining the strength spent by the one, small effort.

In that moment Delilah struggled to place words she knew were not his own. Somewhere behind her, behind this life she had now, she had seen them, read them, in a corner, dark and alone. Then Harold spoke again, "'Are you -- Nobody -- too?'" He nearly trembled from the strain, exhausted, drawing in another great, silent breath. To anyone watching, he'd appear to be in tremendous pain.

But before he could continue, Delilah's memory snapped to. "Emily Dickinson!" she shouted, louder than she had intended but full of the excitement of placing the words of a poet her mother had whispered in her ear as a child, a poet to whom she, herself, was later drawn.

Harold perked at the recognition, his whole body seeming to flourish from an extra surge of blood and adrenaline and he nearly turned to face her.

But instead he only clamped his lips together, stifling both unexpected tears and a bubble of laughter, his eyes wide with the effort of holding both emotions in, and stepped onto the path that led out of the cemetery full of a knowledge that somehow his world was about to change.

When the last of the mourners had left, solemn and quiet, arms wrapped around one another for comfort, seeking strength to understand, Amos crouched beside the headstone and ran his fingers over the letters of Virginia's name. The stone was cold and sent a long, winding chill the length of his arm and down his spine. He hoped some time in the sun would warm it.

"Godspeed, friend," he whispered.

Suddenly the world seemed so full of loss. It seemed that the scattering of headstones spun out into infinity and the whole of the world threatened to spin upside down.

25,000 miles per hour.

In only two years -- Carl, Ellen, now Virginia -- all good people gone too soon.

Too soon.

As Amos tipped his hollow gaze into the clear blueness of the afternoon sky -- blue so pure, so true it seemed to mock him -- his heart bursting with a need to understand and be whole, and as Delilah stood, unseen, a short distance away, poised somewhere between accepting and fleeing, the swans from the pond suddenly soared overhead, silhouetted by the glaring sun, their wings thickly drumming the air as they cast momentary, flickering shadows across the graves. There was such power in their gracefulness that Amos imagined them buoying spirits on their backs, providing passage to a greater beyond.

Suddenly Amos' pain and loneliness grew larger than his capacity to feel them. They stole his strength, taunted his very sense of self, questioning his certainty and bringing him to his knees. He fell heavily against

Virginia's stone. He shook his head, no longer able to make sense of any of it.

In a distant cavern of his mind Amos suddenly heard an echo of Delilah, *"They mate for life..."* and he watched as the swans circled back toward the pond and into the distance like two great angels vanishing into the heavens.

Would that he could have followed Ellen as one swan followed the other. As Virginia followed Carl. As grief followed grief.

Nearby, Delilah made a decision.

"Would you tell me about your dreams, Amos?"

For a brief moment Amos thought it was Ellen, forced back into the world by the intensity of his longing. But when he stood and turned he found Delilah, her green eyes still moist with ghosts of fallen tears. "What?"

"I've just been thinking." She looked at the ground and prodded a clump of grass with the toe of her shoe, feeling a need rising within herself -- foreign and full of power. "And I was wondering if you would tell me about your dreams."

"Dreams?" Amos wiped his eyes with the back of his hand. He hadn't even realized he had been crying.

"Of Ellen."

Amos faltered. "Why?"

"Because -- I don't know. Because -- I'd like to know her...?" It came as a question rather than a statement and she faltered, suddenly uncertain of her reasons, aware of the confusion riding in her chest. "I don't know. Never mind." She turned to leave.

162

"No -- don't go." Amos breathed deeply and turned away from Delilah, away from her piercing gaze, looking instead out across the field of stones and markers and angels -- all set to remain longer than the lives they are built to represent. The eternal weighing heavily down upon the transient in an effort to hold it in place a bit longer.

In spite of all the images and thoughts cascading through his mind in response to Delilah's request he still could not seem to find a way to form the words. Three times his mouth opened to begin, wanting to share the wonder that Ellen had been to him, and three times it closed without uttering a sound. He had lost the connection between thought and speech, lost the path from internal to external, lost his way.

"Did you love her instantly?" Delilah prodded.

"Yes." Amos nodded, still looking off toward the edge of the cemetery, afraid of the sound of his own voice, wishing Delilah would stop, praying she didn't.

"Did you ever hurt her?" She hadn't meant to ask that, certainly not that way, but there it was. Something she needed to understand. There were connections in her mind that didn't quite make sense, things she somehow assumed followed one another and yet didn't naturally match.

"What? Hurt her?" Amos turned toward Delilah, whose gaze instantly dropped to the ground. "No. Never. I loved her." He looked away again. "I love her."

"Are the dreams happy ones?" Delilah's desire grew fierce, her need to comprehend, to know what this love was, what it gave, what it left behind.

Amos paused, a sad smile playing at the corners of his mouth as he focused on something over the tips of the trees. "Bittersweetly, yes. She is *always* laughing and taking my hand. Sometimes—*most* times—I never want to wake up." He turned toward Delilah then, with no conscious thought, and took her hand in his, stroking her fingers as he relived his dreams. "She takes my hand and I can feel the warmth of it against my palm, as well as that of her breath when she leans close to whisper in my ear..."

Once he began, Amos found himself unable to stop the flood of memories. As he and Delilah strolled through the empty paths of the cemetery, he recounted his whole life with Ellen—all the joy and sadness, the depth of their love, and his endless amazement at her very existence. With laughter that tripped through leaves like lilting butterflies, and tears that seemed to shudder the earth, he introduced Delilah to his beloved Ellen, and in the telling felt closer to Ellen that he had in the year and a half since she died.

"You know what it is, Delilah?" Amos paused on the path, lightly touching Delilah's arm. "It's all the small things. Not the big, dramatic events you'd expect to leap forward, but the small, regular moments that string together like pearls and make up a life. Like all the mornings she sat at the table, her hands cupped around a mug of coffee, her head bowed over school papers -- it was nothing special. But I'd walk in and be startled to find her there, you know? I mean, of course I knew she'd be there, but still -- seeing her there each and every morning, confirming what I knew again and again, the simple act of her presence -- it always caught me off guard.

"She'd catch me staring at her full of happy amazement and she'd laugh, touch her hand to her hair and ask, 'What?' She knew 'what.' She knew she floored me just by being there each and every day. But it made her shy. Which only endeared me to her more."

"She sounds wonderful. I wish I'd known her."

Amos looked at Delilah, who appeared so open, so accessible. "She was a lot like you are, really. She could make me laugh completely unexpectedly, showed me things of myself and the world I might otherwise have missed..." He looked away again. Too close. "You are a lot like her."

It was a sad, honest sharing, filled with pain and joy -- good for the strength it gave his memory of Ellen, sad for the reminder that she was, indeed, no more than a memory forever.

"I think," Amos continued after a moment of pause, speaking more to himself than anyone else, "I think that the last days of Ellen's life was the first time I truly felt how much I loved her. The first time I understood the depth and completeness of that love. As though what I'd felt before was only a pale shadow of true, boundless love.

"The moment I understood -- in my bones -- that I was about to lose her, only then did love, my love for her, become clear.

"I think that's how it works. You never have an honest, real sense of love, of what that means, to love someone, until you are threatened with its loss.

"Only then."

Delilah thought of those last moments with her mother -- the touch of her fingertips, the dullness of her gaze -- and tried to recall if she experienced a sudden comprehension of their love.

Perhaps she had been too young.

Perhaps she had never loved her mother at all. There hadn't been much room, after all. Fear, terror, and shame require a great deal of space and do not concern themselves with leaving room for love.

"You're very lucky, Amos, to have had someone like her. And she's lucky to have someone like you to remember her."

Amos hadn't felt lucky in nearly two years, but as they passed beneath the stone archway that marked the entrance to the cemetery he glanced at Delilah, who lifted her hand in the air toward a passing monarch butterfly, its flutter of orange and black seeming to pause and take notice of something distinct before lighting on her perfectly still, outstretched finger in an occurrence as impossible as a fairy appearing there. She held it near her face, cooing softly about its beauty, as though the creature displayed some kind of insecurity that demanded her reassurance, and with each gentle strain of exhalation its wings softly closed and opened as if to say, "Yes, I hear you...".

And Amos thought, *Perhaps I am very lucky after all.*

After leaving Amos and the cemetery, Delilah returned to what was now her home and walked through the empty space. She stood in the kitchen and saw Virginia everywhere—at the sink washing vegetables, at the table drinking coffee.

In the living room Virginia stood at the window, sat curled on the couch with a glass of iced tea

Delilah climbed the stairs, her fingers tracing a path in the cherry banister that Virginia's fingers had followed a thousand times. Cobwebs she'd never noticed before hung in the corners and a damp draft curled through hallways and skimmed along walls like ethereal snakes slinking through garden paths. Each creaking floorboard put a sound to the emptiness as though the house, itself, felt something lacking.

In Virginia's room, she stood at the foot of the bed as the breeze billowed the curtains in pregnant wafts, and she tried to feel as at home as when Virginia had been there.

It wasn't the same.

A hollowness rang throughout that Delilah imagined echoing forever.

She'd learned long ago that it wasn't a house that made a home, but rather the people inside it.

The people inside.

Sitting on the edge of the bed, hearing the old joints and springs creaking with age, she lay back atop the coverlet and let the silence wash over her. She had been alone before. She's *always* been alone. Alone was something she knew how to do.

At least she used to.

Had that changed?

Later, as the afternoon fell toward dusk, in the thin, diffused light, Harold watched Delilah step out onto the front porch, arms wrapped around herself as though she were cold, even though the day was still muggy and warm.

On the floor just outside the door lay the book of Emily Dickinson poems which she stooped to retrieve. She smiled, looking out toward the road and the woods to see if the giver of the gift was still nearby. But there was no one. No one she could see. Harold was too adept to be spotted as he cowered in the woods across the street behind the trunk of a giant oak tree, his index finger entwined in a stray curl of hair.

The rain had brought mosquitoes that darted around Delilah as she stood on the porch. She flipped through the book of poems but a lone mockingbird bathing in a puddle at the foot of the steps distracted her. After a round of rinsing, he flew up to a maple branch to belt out a myriad of tunes --warbles to screeches to trills -- none of which he could legitimately call his own, then back to the puddle he went for another pass at dunking and splashing. It made Delilah laugh. He was a silly bird, stealing songs with bravado and claiming them for himself without apology, his long, slim tail twitching and jerking as he sang. It may have been serious work, whatever he was doing, but to Delilah he looked full of pride and play, a freedom and abandon she wished she could feel. Even once.

Virginia's rocker, the old cane-backed chair she sat in every evening, stood woefully empty in front of the living room window. Delilah walked over to it and gave it a little push, then stepping back to the porch railing, she leaned against the column and watched the steady movement rocking... rocking.

Just when she thought it must be running out of steam from such a gentle push, it would swing forward and back once more, determined, it seemed, to continue on forever now that it had been set in motion.

Over the next few days Amos discovered that the storm on the day of Virginia's departure had taken its toll throughout the town. Millie lost some stock to water damage—colored felt, ribbons and lace stained and wilted; a portion of farmers' crops were waterlogged. But nothing seemed as permanent as the change to the pond. It looked as though it might never return to normal, leaving the gazebo stranded—an island shelter.

The bog that had begun at the onset of the storm had evolved into a legitimate addition to the existing pond. Water levels rose, run-off flooded, and what remained was an extension of shallow waters that enclosed the forlorn gazebo, making it inaccessible to all but frogs, birds, and the swans who appeared to be building a nest along its rail.

Amos stood at the new edge of the pond, stared at the stranded gazebo, and thought about how all the planning in the world couldn't completely insulate or protect you from the unexpected. Those who planned the park and designed the pond and gazebo did not expect that it would ever end up so... isolated. But it had, and everyone else would simply have to adapt.

That's what life was, after all -- a constant series of adaptations.

Knowing that, however, did not make it any easier.

He missed Virginia already and thought of something Delilah had said not long after her arrival as they sat at his counter in the early morning quiet, "Oh, this world, Amos. There are so many reasons to hate it, to want to damn it for eternity. And yet... I love it. I didn't used to, but I do now. I love everything about it even though I don't know why."

The day seemed to linger, the sun almost unwilling to set, only forlornly relinquishing dusk to early evening after a magnificent, fiery battle along the horizon.

Delilah watched it from the water tower that stood across the road from the edge of Carver's Park woods and overlooked the railroad tracks—an old, fairly small, wooden tower, long unused, the boards slowly baking and warping in the summer sun. The roof was out of the question since the storm; Amos would be looking for her there. It wasn't private any longer.

But this—the gallery that encircled the edge of the tower—easily took the roof's place. Indeed, rising higher than the pitch of Virginia's roof it became Rapunzel's tower from which she never wanted rescuing, affording greater distance between herself and the sometimes unbearable pull of the earth beneath her feet. Distance between herself and the weight of a sometimes unruly world. Rising above ground level provided a view that reminded her -- of what? Of goodness, awe, serenity. Silent breezes tickling the tops of the trees sent a slow tremble down the length of the branches; the cold, cobalt twilight created a sky of blown glass full of sparkling, shining points of distant, untouchable light.

Leaning her elbows on the railing, fingers drumming the dry wood with hundreds of feet between herself and the ground, she felt a lilt in her stomach tugging at her, like a rabbit she'd once seen caught in a trap tugging for freedom. A lilt that seemed to be responding to the easy breeze fingering her curls, and the swallows that fluttered through twilight shadows. It seemed a longing born before her own life and carried nestled, tethered within the furthermost corners of her soul.

It was something she only came close to glimpsing while deeply entangled in rare, liberating dreams.

A train whistle blew, startling her, and she listened as the echo faded into the quiet evening, riding spiraling drafts upward into cold, dense space.

From her perch she saw beyond the top of the tree line, an enormous length of track extending in both directions. Origin and destination (past and future?). The water tower loomed over the point in the track that was Now. That's where she stood. Always and forever. Here. Now. Past and Future simply far-away dreams.

Far below, at the small, white circle that was the gazebo, Delilah saw Virginia Emmett standing on the steps, flanked by the two swans, and staring at the murky waters of the surrounding pond. The diffused light of dusk skipped along the shifting surface in winking dapples, and as Delilah watched, the figure looked up and waved, smile as warm and as radiant as ever, the soft spill of early moonlight reflecting off her skin.

Delilah gripped the railing as a wave of vertigo rushed over her, through her, her heart catching on something sharp, pausing as if to gather its thoughts. But then a gentle breeze full of lavender and warm apple muffins slowly enveloped her like a soft, wool blanket in winter. She smiled, waving in return, while Virginia turned to climb the last few steps into the gazebo, just as the train suddenly sped past, rattling the ground far below.

The world is full of more than we can imagine.

For the first time in her life, Delilah didn't just remember her mother, she longed for her. She longed to have her here, now, not just a distant, fading memory.

Amos made a half-hearted meal which he half-ate while half-watching mindless primetime television, spent an hour standing on the front porch with his hands in his pockets, and then thoughtlessly climbed into a bed that seemed to grow minutely larger with each passing day. Larger and emptier.

He dreamed more that night than he had in a long while -- whirling, kaleidoscopic images that mixed people, places and times in ways that were untrue and yet, in essence, more accurate than reality.

Ellen followed throughout, always a short caress away, always appearing with a loving, reassuring touch on his shoulder, freckled cheeks smiling, hazel eyes glowing with unearthly warmth.

It wasn't until he awoke close to morning that he realized the radiant, young woman that appeared with Ellen, her long, dusty brown hair clipped loosely atop her head, had been Virginia. As she once was. As she appeared in old, faded photos before time and experience left their indelible marks. As she would eternally be.

The women in his life have been truly remarkable. He has, indeed, been lucky. But he has also lost those remarkable women. All except Delilah. Suddenly all his faith in life, his reason, fell to her. He did not realize it, but Delilah had become his world, and he latched onto her, the idea of her, the real, living truth of her in a way that almost put her in peril. Surely if you direct that much force, that much dependence on one element of support, the bridge will collapse.

But Delilah was stronger than that, stronger than him, than all of them. Wasn't she?

*A*mos decided to open the store late the next morning, reluctant to release the images that lingered when he first awoke, hoping that if he remained in bed, replaying them over and over in an ever faster loop, they might—like a centrifuge—solidify and prove to be more than ghosts of dreams. But it failed. Still all he was left with was a pain around his empty heart, echoes in an empty house, too much room in a half-empty bed full of sheets twisted and gnarled, somehow smelling of her no matter how many times he had washed them. And finally, for real, he cried. Not gentle, sad tears, but crushing sobs that stole his breath and burned his throat. Tears so full they demanded a voice, refusing to fall silently, forcing audible, coughing sounds from deep in his lungs. Eighteen months of holding back, pushing down, and making believe finally culminated into a twister of emotions all black and raging and out of control. It pressed him deeply into pillows, beneath blankets, curling him around himself until his knees touched his chest, his arms wrapped his legs and the torrent of tears pooled in the creases of his elbows and the curves of his ear.

The abyss grew wider, the despair larger, his spirit slipping ever deeper. This torrent was stronger than he was. Stronger than he wanted to be. So he gave up all notion of struggle or resistance and relinquished himself to the pull of sorrow.

And in the end, the very act of surrender released him. His breathing slowed, his sobs quieted and finally, he could cry no more.

The bed, the house, his heart, remained empty. Nothing rushed in to fill the vacuum that he'd been denying. There were no angels, or horns, or epiphanies. But when he finally got up and dressed, although his head ached and his spirit was tired, both were also surprisingly clear and light, swept clean by the storm. And he found Delilah waiting on his front porch.

"She loved you, you know. In her own way." She sat on the steps, toes of her sneakers touching as though her feet had been put on crooked, shielding the sun from her eyes with her hand as she looked up at him.

As he rolled up his sleeves, he moved so he stood as a shade for her. "Who?"

"Virginia."

Sometimes when Delilah spoke, so simply, so directly, it chilled him. There were things she said that didn't seem to come from her. Or shouldn't be able to. Things she spoke with such clarity and certainty that it unnerved him.

No one could be *that* sure of anything. Not even that the sun would rise each morning. You just never know.

"Is that so?" He turned and went down the steps. Delilah followed.

"As a matter of fact it is, yes."

"Delilah..." Just outside the gate Amos turned toward her. Her eyes shone so clear, so honest, that looking at her made him dizzy and he suddenly forgot what he had wanted to say. "Care to walk with me to the store?"

She smiled. "I'd love to. It looks like it's going to be a beautiful day."

"Oh, and by the way, good morning."

"Good morning, Amos," Delilah replied, smiling.

Amos had noticed an unusual quietness in the town the past few days as people felt the loss of Virginia.

When people spoke, they did so softly, whispering of life's frailty and uncertainty. They sat closer, talked more openly, fought less.

For a while, it seemed to Amos, there was a real reverence for life.

Then that started to change. Kate Harnett and Sarah Martinson stopped in for coffee, and Amos overheard them talking about the fact that Virginia left him the house, their voices hushed not in reverence but in gossip.

Then Millie came in and joined their conversation, commenting that it looked like Delilah had a place to stay as long as she liked.

It was nothing more than typical, idle banter, its importance stemming from the fact that it signaled a return to normalcy.

Delilah had parted ways with Amos on Main Street, heading to the farmer's market in the opposite direction. She loved to walk through the open air market and lose herself in the sweet, earthy aromas of fresh peaches and sweet corn, melons and rhubarb.

She bought some plums and soft, sweet peaches and left the coolness of the market. As she stepped onto the sidewalk, the contrast of shade to sun blinding her, she collided with Harold Reinman. The stack of books he carried tumbled to the ground.

"Oh, God! I'm so sorry!" She scrambled to help him retrieve the books from the dusty soil.

Now that she could clearly see his face, he looked to be in his mid-twenties. He never quite looked her in the eye, nearly avoided her altogether. His hands shook, and he seemed to move toward her and away from her at the same time. She could feel his nerves, his need, his fear. Then Delilah saw a shift in him. He stilled and said, "'Hope is the thing with feathers...'" He paused, waiting.

Delilah looked at him, not sure of his meaning.

Harold tried again, saying each word clearly and distinctly, "'Hope is the thing with feathers...'" He trailed off in an obvious effort to prompt her.

She clenched her jaw, suddenly understanding that he wanted her to fill in the next line, a poem from the collection he'd left her and one she had once tacked to her mirror and read every day for almost a year. It surprised her, excited her, his tentative attempt. "'That perches in the soul/And sings the tune without words...'" she paused, allowing Harold to finish.

"'And never stops -- at all...'"

And in unison, as though it had been planned as such all along, "Emily Dickinson."

Delilah smiled and breathed deeply as Harold simply gathered his books from the ground, his tangle of brown curls falling in his eyes, and with only a brief, almost non-existent glance toward her, stood and continued down Main Street, one sneaker untied, half a denim shirt-tail untucked from the waist.

A woman who worked at the market appeared beside her. "That's Harold Reinman."

"Yes. I know." Delilah was almost laughing, giddy.

"Such a sad story. Bright boy when he was young, and sweet as anything. Then his mother took one too many swings at him, knocked him down the cellar stairs and then killed herself. He was in a coma for a long time, and that's how it left him. They say he's got no real sense of the world around him. Not really."

"And the books?" Delilah still watched as Harold's figure grew smaller and smaller in the distance, hovering within the heatwave mirages on the pavement. She felt the rush of anticipation, a sense of something looming, just out of reach, but waiting. Waiting.

"I guess he reads them all. The library lets him take a stack out a month at a time, and like clockwork every month he returns one bunch and gets another. He lives in his mother's house back that way." The woman pointed behind them down Main Street where the woods began to grow thick. "Seems to do okay, I guess. Amos Harrison brings him groceries and such regularly. You're Delilah, aren't you?"

Delilah did not reply. She stared at Harold's diminishing image, the heat mirage reflecting him, making him shimmer and appear unsubstantial. Ignoring the woman who returned to the market, she watched him more intensely than at the funeral, and without distraction. And in the way that pain recognizes pain, loneliness knows loneliness, in the way that looking in a mirror shows a reflection of yourself, Delilah saw something when she had looked Harold in the eye. She saw something in the way he held his shoulders close as though trying to make himself smaller, the way he took her in, but only in quick, sideways glances, the way he unobtrusively avoided touching, even for an instant. In all those things she glimpsed the familiar and she didn't know whether to laugh or cry. "He knows," Delilah said softly to no one. "He knows."

At sixteen Delilah had ceased to speak.

For weeks she moved through the world in silence, and although the behavior fueled her father's rage and increased the episodes of violence, Delilah found the silence to be protective, insular, so that the blows, when they came, fell painlessly as though every nerve in her body had died. She would stare at the resulting scrapes and bruises with curiosity, seeing the anger in them, marveling at how, even if she were to press a finger deep into a bluish-purple mark on her arm, she felt nothing.

Nothing.

Leaving the farmer's market, Delilah knew precisely where to go for answers.

"Amos, tell me about Harold Reinman." She began the conversation before she was fully inside the door. The store was empty save for Amos who was brewing a fresh pot of coffee.

"If you're asking me about him, you must already know." He finished filling the coffee maker and leaned on the counter near Delilah who sat wiping a film of sweat from her forehead with a napkin.

She smiled. "I suppose I do. Some. I know that he reads a lot and doesn't tie his sneakers. But I wanted to hear it from you." She leaned forward against the counter. Its coolness seemed to invite her to lie down on the Formica.

Amos sighed and straightened, folding his large arms across his chest. "Well, he never had a father that I know of, and his mother—and I use the term loosely— should've taken off as well, as far as I'm concerned. Beat the hell out of the boy one too many times, basically."

"Then killed herself."

"Too bad she didn't do that first." His gaze flicked briefly to her scars. "Not that I'd really wish that for anyone..."

"I know you wouldn't, Amos. Not you. Frankly, I agree. And he lives on his own?"

"Not at first, he didn't. But he kept taking off back to his house -- God knows why, with all the horror he lived through there -- and by the fourth time everyone was so fed up they were talking about locking him up. I told them that if they let him live at his house I'd keep an eye on him, so they let him go."

"Just like that?"

"Yeah, well, frankly nobody really seemed to want to be bothered. All they saw was a hopeless case who was a pain in the ass. I saw a boy who wanted to go home."

"So Amos came to the rescue..." Delilah suddenly saw something different in Amos, a softness unlike the one for his wife or Virginia.

"Well..."

"This is a *good* thing, Amos."

"Yeah, well... do you mind if I ask why the interest?"

"No, I don't mind." She sat quietly, wryly, waiting.

Amos coughed up a short laugh. "Okay, miss smartass, why the interest?"

"Your eyes sparkle when you laugh, Amos. You should do it more often. I saw him today on his way to the library. I have a feeling about him."

"A feeling, eh?" Amos poured himself a cup of coffee. An unfamiliar couple came in and scanned the shelves. Travelers. The rare kind that looked quick enough to notice a town they could stop in. "What sort of feeling?"

"That he's not as unaware as people say."

"Virginia said that too." Amos raised his coffee cup as an offering to her.

"No thanks. I'm off to the library." She rose from her seat as the couple moved to the register with their items.

"Not working today, Delilah?" He spoke as he rang up their sodas and snacks.

"Nope!" she called on her way out, "I called out 'Well'!" And a trail of laughter trickled behind her, infecting Amos and the couple at the counter.

"Called out well," Amos muttered, then looked up to the young couple. "She probably did."

A few seconds after Delilah left, Jack Gruffen pulled the Dodge to a stop outside Amos' store. As he climbed from the driver's seat, he squinted down the road at the back of a young girl with copper ringlets of hair. For a moment his heart seemed to skip a beat, but then he reminded himself he'd been seeing red-headed girls all along his trip—both real and imagined. He was not so quick to trust what he saw now.

Flicking his cigarette to the dirt, he entered the store. He strolled the aisles a moment, trying to get a feel for the place and for the large, black man standing behind the counter. He wanted to know what might make this place special. A place to go to when you were leaving someplace else. Someone else. Then he grabbed a bag of chips and disposable razors and set them at the cash register.

"Hello," Amos said. "Can I get you anything else?"

"Nope, this is it." Jack mustered up a smile.

"Where you headed?" Amos asked as he rang up Jack's items.

"Nowhere, really. Just exploring. I've never seen this part of the country." Jack had spoken the line so many times already it had begun to sound like the truth.

"Well, it's a pretty part, that's for sure." Amos paused as he pulled out a bag for the chips and razors. "And suddenly very popular. Folks don't usually stop here—the town's easy to miss—but we had a couple pass through just a few minutes ago, now you. Hell, we even had one a few months ago who got off a bus and moved in!" He stopped, embarrassed. His uneasiness with strangers always caused one of two reactions: either he couldn't say anything, or he babbled about nothing.

Jack clenched his jaw and pulled a rubber band from his pocket, wrapping it around his index finger until the tip turned blue. "Is that so? Just moved right in?"

"Yup, I don't know if she meant to or not, but here's where she stopped, and here's where she stayed."

Jack's head began to throb. "Well, I'll be damned. Must be a helluva town!" He invoked his best regular-joe-shooting-the-breeze smile.

"We think so." Amos smiled, thinking he saw something familiar in the man.

"Well, you certainly seem friendly enough, I'll give you that much." Jack smiled again and paid for his things. "Thanks very much."

"Sure thing. Enjoy the rest of your trip."

"I will. Thanks." Jack paused, "Hey, if I wanted to stay here for a few days, where could I get a room?"

Amos looked up at Jack. "You'd have to go into Sinclair, next town over."

"Really? Nothing here at all?"

"Well, there's the Emmett's on Ellington Street, but they only have one room to rent, and that's taken. Plus, the owner recently passed away."

"Oh. I'm sorry to hear that." Jack fought the nervous jiggle in his right leg. He was anxious to move on.

"Yeah, well. That's life, right? We're born, we live, we die."

"So it is." Jack pushed open the door. "Well, thanks again!" He stepped back out into the afternoon sun and slid back into the sweltering car. He shook a cigarette from the pack he kept stuck behind the sun visor. The Emmett's. That shouldn't be hard to find. Perhaps this whole ordeal was nearly over.

It was just before noon, but the day had already grown hot enough for the library's dark coolness to seem a vast mountain cave, a glade amidst an arid desert.

Delilah had no way of knowing for certain if Harold would still be there, but she hoped he took his time choosing his month's-worth of reading. She hoped one of the things they shared was their discovery of safe places; library walls are high and thick, the shelves close and concealing, aisles cool and quiet. A rich serenity brewed there, the weight and breadth of history and imagination rushing into lungs, stealing speech, leaving silence.

"Hi. Can I help you with anything?" Kate Harnett smiled from behind the desk.

Delilah paused. "Maybe. I'm actually looking for Harold Reinman, if you've seen him."

"Really? Harold?" Kate took a moment, her blond brows furrowed, as though expecting more from Delilah. "He should be that way." She pointed past the center tables to the stacks beyond.

"Thanks." Delilah smiled and crossed the main floor, feeling Kate's curious gaze at her back. Her sneakers squeaked on the marble as she strolled the aisles, mindlessly scanning book bindings, breathing in the musty smell of old pages and use.

She found Harold in the science fiction/fantasy section, a library cart beside him with two books on it: Fritz Leiber and William Gibson. He stood close to the bookshelf, his finger trailing the bindings as though he read the titles through his fingertips. Then he'd stop, pull a book from the shelf, hunch over it as he flipped it open, scan the first few pages, return the book to its place and continue on.

She watched him for nearly ten minutes during which time he covered an entire section of shelves, returning twice to previous spots without hesitation to retrieve a book and place it on the cart.

As he moved to History, Delilah followed, quietly observing his studied process -- always the same sequence -- until another book found its way to the cart. A half hour passed, during which time other borrowers had come and gone, their quiet conversation an ebbing and flowing of soft, hypnotic whispers.

At the end of the aisle Harold paused, turning slowly to Delilah. He lifted his face, looking at her eye to eye -- just looking -- a moment that stretched like unreachable escape routes in nightmares, then suddenly he smiled. It lasted no more than a breath, was perhaps only an illusion, before he turned back to the cart and continued on his way.

Just one, brief, moment.

But it was all Delilah needed.

She laughed to herself. "I knew it," she sighed. "I knew it."

Leaving the library and Harold, Delilah strolled over to the water tower. The sun burned fiercely but a breeze blowing from the north raised goosebumps on her skin each time the sun ducked behind a cloud.

For a moment she stood at the foot of the ladder, craning her neck back to look to the top, the sun radiating behind the tower, creating a monstrous silhouette. A castle in the sky. Or a wicker man.

She got sunspots in her eyes that made her dizzy.

"I know who you are." A male voice from behind startled her, momentarily. She lurched forward and struck her forehead on the ladder.

"Shit!" She whirled, on the defensive, to find Harold, six books balanced in his arms. "Harold! Christ, you scared the hell out of me!" She sat on the grass in Harold's shadow.

"I know who you are," he repeated.

Delilah rubbed the knot rising on her forehead, wincing at the sharp stab she felt. "Well, good. Then we're even aren't we?"

"You're Delilah." Harold rocked from foot to foot like a stiff-legged soldier.

"And you're Harold."

Harold stood a moment as Delilah tended her bruise, waiting silently for her to feel him watching and raise her eyes to his. He held the books tightly to his chest and continued his mesmerizing rocking, his lips repeating an endless string of silent words. When she finally took notice he spoke again, "'When all the blandishments of life are gone/The coward sneaks to death, the brave live on.' George Sewell. 'The Suicide.'"

Then he smiled again, that same, ingenuous, honest smile and turned, setting off toward home. "Goodbye, Delilah!" he called.

More than a little bewildered, and somehow full of laughter Delilah replied, "See ya, Harold," and decided to forego the long climb up the tower in favor of simply lying back in the grass hoping the heat of the sun would magically melt the bump over her right eyebrow. Sometimes the surprises life threw were pleasant ones.

Harold took a detour on his way back home, circling back toward Amos' store. He was certain now that Delilah was different. He'd had a sense of it the first time he saw her outside Virginia's house, felt more certain at the cemetery in the moment he took a chance. Then, in the library he had turned toward her in an instant of defiance, prepared to dare her, perhaps even warn her, since he was still full of uncertain fear, but when he looked at her, something inside him quieted. She didn't make him nervous. In fact, she did just the opposite.

Delilah.

Outside Amos', he went to the soda machine.

He'd forgotten a lot of things since his accident, wished he'd forgotten others; but the one thing he was glad he remembered was the money he'd been hiding since he was a boy. Money he made by working odd jobs around town. Anything to avoid going home. He saved it, hid it beneath the porch for when he finally became old enough to leave. To run away. Unfortunately the hospital and the forgetting came before then, and so now the money became his treat stash. Sodas and ice cream, when they weren't given as a gift, were paid for out of his savings in small, loose change. He didn't need it very often.

Setting his books on the bench, he fed the soda machine a few quarters, pushed the orange-soda button and retrieved the can when it clunked down.

"Can you get out of the way now, freak boy?"

Turning, Harold faced Sam Cooper standing silently beside a boy he didn't recognize, neither more than thirteen years old. The one who had spoken stepped forward and gave Harold a little push even though Harold was at least a foot taller. When Harold didn't respond, the boy pushed him again, harder this time, sending Harold down onto the bench beside the machine.

"Hey!" Amos appeared in the doorway to the store and addressed the boys. "If you're going to behave that way your money's no good here. So Harold can stand in front of that machine all day if he wants."

Sam stared at the ground silently. He liked Amos. His cousin was a smartass and Sam knew he shouldn't have pointed Harold out on their way by.

Amos stepped out of the store. "Sam, what do you think your folks would have to say?"

"I'm sorry, Mr. Harrison. We're going." He turned to leave, tugging his cousin's shirt sleeve for him to follow.

Harold hadn't moved, only watched with his eyes as the boys ran off, then took a long drink of his soda.

Amos came to his side. "You okay there, Harold? Anything you need besides that soda?"

Harold turned toward Amos, a rare occurrence in itself, but then went a step further by fixing him with a stare focused and intense -- the polar opposite of his usual vacant, empty glances. It actually made Amos catch his breath as though Harold had reached out and touched his soul.

"Delilah," Harold said.

Then he simply gathered his books from the bench and headed home leaving Amos scratching his neck and thinking, *What the hell is going on in that boy's head?*

Jack followed Amos' directions and found a Howard Johnson's Motor Lodge just outside Sinclair. He figured he'd hole up for a few days, maybe a week, get some rest and decide how he should proceed. This had to be done right, and for once he was going to try to adhere to that.

The girl behind the counter was young, with light, strawberry blonde hair cut like a boy's. She reminded him... he suddenly broke out in a sweat, his stomach burned and his throat tightened. He clenched his jaw against the spin in his gut and concentrated on signing his name.

"Is everything okay?" the girl asked, her voice small and sweet. It made his teeth hurt, like too much sugar.

Jack nodded and smiled. "Yeah. Fine. Just the heat, I guess." Taking his room key he left the office, got in the car, and drove around the back to number twenty-seven.

Once inside, he tossed his bag on the bed and headed for the bathroom. He splashed cold water on his face and looked at himself in the mirror; bags under his eyes, skin sallow, he had meant to shave before leaving the last motel but forgot and now had nearly a week's growth. The only reason he didn't mind was that the beard covered most of the scar on his left cheek. He faced that scar every day, recalling his fourteenth birthday, his father's eyes as he let the knife fly, the blood soaking his new white shirt. Normally he felt the reminder was a good one, but right now he was tired and just wanted some peace.

Leaving the bathroom he collapsed on the chair by the bed, his head in his hands, forehead damp with a thin film of sweat.

The tears that came surprised him; he'd been numb to them for so long. But having gone two days without a drink, wanting to be clear-headed and composed—wanting to do this right—left him vulnerable. He suddenly found himself full of loss, and a deep, hard ache. He missed his wife, Lorraine, long since pulled from the river where she dove deep and tied herself to submerged roots, filling her lungs with silt and water. She was long gone, beyond his reach, beyond return.

But that wasn't true of all things, and he didn't want to be alone. That didn't seem too much to ask. Was it?

190

Alone made him thoughtful, sorrowful, too full of things he didn't want.

Lifting his head he found his reflection in the dresser mirror. It was his father, eyes red-rimmed and full of nothing. Pupils dense, dark holes—an entrance into a bottomless, cold void. He hated that face, that weak, empty look, and knew only one way to rid himself of it. Just a little. Not enough to bring on the fog, just a nip to dispel the vision. The ache. Just a sip to chase the ghosts away.

When Delilah opened her eyes again, rising slowly from murky sleep-thoughts and feeling she had crossed galaxies, the sun had slipped low in the sky, casting long, inky blue shadows across the field. Across the road the white swans glowed incandescent in the surrounding dimness, two ethereal figures on the glassy surface of the pond.

She started home, a dull ache spreading across her skull, and when she touched the bump over her eye she knew there was a slight bruise. Probably a hint of blue with an undertone of red. She considered herself lucky she didn't split her head open.

When she reached Haven Lane, she saw Amos who stopped and waited for her to catch up.

"Enjoy the day, Delilah? It was a good one to have off." They walked side by side along the shaded road.

"Hmm. Yeah, I did." She glanced up at him and smiled carefully.

Amos stopped, a hand on her arm pulling her to a stop as well. "Whoa! That's quite a knock on your brow! Are you okay?"

"Yeah. Just got taken by surprise." She paused. "By Harold Reinman, in fact."

Amos' face dropped. "Jesus. He didn't do that to you, did he? I mean, they always said..."

"No!" She placed both hands on his arms, feeling the tension instantly release. "Oh, God, no." She coaxed him into walking again. As they passed Millie's house, Rufus the cat made a few quick passes around their legs before darting off into the woods. "No. He just snuck up behind me, and when he spoke, it scared the hell out of me and I cracked my head. Graceful, huh?"

"He spoke to you? Like a conversation?"

"Well, I don't know if I'd go that far, but we exchanged words."

"Harold hasn't spoken a word to anyone in years. Well, a word maybe, but not much more." Again Amos wondered what was happening with Harold.

"I told you I had a feeling about him," Delilah said as they turned the corner onto Ellington.

"So you did."

A barn owl called into the twilight -- once, twice, three times -- leaving Amos with a hollow feeling rolling around inside. One he feared would follow him into sleep, bending dreams into nightmares.

"Just be careful, Delilah. I love Harold, but I don't think we can be sure of what's inside him. You know?"

She paused at the gate to the Emmett house, one hand atop the pickets, the other propped on her hip. So much passed across her face from youthful tenderness to elder bemusement that for a brief moment Amos witnessed the gamut of what Delilah was capable of. "Don't you worry about me, Amos. I'll be just fine. You know, you would have made a terrific father." Then turning, she ran through the gate, human again, bounded up the porch steps, and disappeared into the quiet safety of the house.

Amos remained just a moment, trying to grab onto some familiar sense of himself, wrestling with Delilah's last comment, then he turned toward his own house, leaving just a moment too soon to see the owl light on the eave of the roof, its eyes glowing ethereally in the dusk.

*A*fter a dinner eaten alone in a kitchen still full of Virginia's perfumes and aromas all permanently absorbed into cracks in the floor, soaked into the wood, enmeshed in the curtains, Delilah sat on the porch in Virginia's rocker, an ice pack held against her forehead. Only eighteen, but the soft creak of the rocking chair, the chirp of invisible crickets, and the fatigue creeping up on her all conspired to make her feel five times that.

But the night had grown deep and cool in contrast to the oppressive day, and the drop in temperature seemed to ease the steady ache in her head. She could have gone to have it looked at, but she knew—in the same way geologists knew slate from limestone and entomologists knew this beetle from that one—she knew it would amount to nothing but a tender spot and a day or two of headaches.

She had noticed Harold lurking across the street nearly fifteen minutes ago but waited to see if he might actually step out of the shadows on his own.

He didn't. Which didn't surprise her since she knew that was where Harold lived, in the shadows just out of sight, out on the fringes of the inhabited world. He occupied a place somewhere between our world and the abyss, nimbly straddling the line, able to traverse back and forth at will. Not that he willed it often. The grey area in between held him safe. She understood that.

"Why don't you come up here and sit down, Harold?"

His lanky figure emerged like a spirit from the shadows of a maple tree, perhaps from the tree itself, a remnant of ancient beliefs and powers, and Delilah watched as he loped slowly through the gate and up the porch steps, only then solidifying into a corporeal being.

"I didn't want to scare you again," he said.

"Well, I appreciate that. Sit down." She gestured to a chair beside her. As he set down a handful of books and lowered himself into the chair, Delilah thought that while he might be around twenty-five or twenty-seven, his mother's blow had knocked parts of him somewhere back into his childhood.

Harold glanced quickly at her. "I'm sorry for the bump on your head."

"It's okay. Look." She removed the ice pack. "Nearly gone. And it was just an accident. I know that."

"Okay. Good. I'm glad you're okay. That's good."

She watched as his right hand stayed in nearly constant motion, brushing his nose, his hair, fingering

195

his jeans, scratching his neck. It moved like a moth, flitting from point to point, pausing a fraction of a second before moving on, white and shuddering.

They sat quietly for a while, Delilah listening to cricket songs and peep frogs, watching the occasional bat flutter through the twilight like a drunken sparrow.

"'Tell me not in mournful numbers,'" Harold began softly, his gaze distant and straight ahead, "'Life is but an empty dream!/For the soul is dead that slumbers/And things are not what they seem.' Henry W. Longfellow, *A Psalm for Life*." He looked around the porch. "I liked Mrs. Emmett." He paused, as though startled by the sound of his voice suddenly coming loudly in the quiet darkness, as if he hadn't spoken moments before. "She was always really nice to me."

"Was she?" Delilah studied Harold, looking for the link between who he was now and the quoting Harold of the previous instant. There seemed many different Harolds, all tucked away in their own compartments, stepping forward only when the moment called for them.

"Yeah. She'd come visit sometimes and bring cookies and muffins—right from the oven!"

"Yup. That's Virginia."

"Do you miss her?" Harold glanced at her out of the corner of his eye.

"Yes. I do. Very much." Although sometimes she couldn't find the place in her that felt the loss. Already it dimmed. Sometimes she stood at the stove cooking pasta, or turned back the bedspread, smoothing wrinkles, and felt nothing but quiet emptiness—almost as though she'd always been alone. In that house. That was how it had always been.

"Do you get lonely here?" He looked at his sneakers.

"Not really."

"Oh." He looked defeated.

"However, it is sometimes nice to have someone to sit on the porch with after dinner."

"I could come by sometimes and sit with you!"

Delilah smiled and rocked gently in her chair. "You got a deal there, Harold. Anytime you want."

Harold grinned, and brushing a curl out of his eye, pulled a book from the small pile and settled in for the evening.

Delilah glanced at the books scattered at his feet and rose from her chair. "Don't go away, Harold. I'll be right back."

Harold lifted his nose from his book, eyebrows raised. "Where are you going?"

Delilah paused at the front door. "I'll be right back. I've got something for you."

"For me? A present?" His eyes grew wide.

"You could say that." Delilah stepped inside, leaving Harold to sit impatiently, one leg jiggling.

In moments she returned, handing him her backpack, now empty. She wondered if it meant she was staying on. Or at least that she wasn't leaving. "Here. So you don't have to lug books around in your arms."

Harold took the bag. Turning it over in his hands he peered inside it, sank his arms in to explore its emptiness, opened and closed the outside pockets, all the while wearing an immense, toothy grin. "Wow! This is great!"

Together they gathered the pile of books and arranged them carefully in the pack. Then Harold paused, looked to Delilah and said, "Thanks. So—we're friends?"

Something in the simple innocence of it, the way it was asked not out of concern that it might not be true, but just to secure it, brought tears to Delilah's eyes. "Yeah, Harold. We are definitely friends."

Amos, out for a walk in the comfortable evening, stopped when he heard voices on Virginia's porch. One was Delilah, he was sure of that, the other was less clear save for that it was male.

Glancing past the hydrangea at the corner of Virginia's yard, Amos was surprised to see Harold sitting on the porch talking rapidly with Delilah.

He squinted, blinked and rubbed his neck, but when he looked again it was still Harold. Talking. To Delilah.

"Well I'll be a son of a bitch," he whispered.

Rather than passing the house he walked back the way he'd come, not wanting either of them to feel spied upon.

But no one would believe it. Harold Reinman. Amos laughed, quietly at first, then louder as he moved farther away from Virginia's until he was standing alone in the darkness whooping and clapping his hands.

Hearing an odd sound in the distance, Delilah and Harold paused in their conversation. Delilah shook her head and smiled. "You've got some odd birds in this town, I think."

Harold smiled at his sneakers. "Yup. Odd birds."

Jack Gruffen spent several days getting clean and sober. He got a haircut, shaved his beard, and ate three square meals a day.

Finally feeling almost human, he got in the Dodge Dart and drove back into Macaenas, back onto Main Street, stopping once at the newsstand to ask directions to the Emmett house.

He talked to himself as he drove, trying to calm his nerves. He asked his palms to quit sweating because he didn't want to say hello after all this time with hot, damp palms. He checked the rearview mirror and wished he'd gotten a little more sleep. His eyes were still a little bloodshot, and the dark circles beneath them showed like bruises.

Turning the corner onto Stafford Street, like the directions said, he saw the house. Immense and yellow it burst on his brain, so bright it made him squint. "*That's it,*" he thought. *That's where she is."*

His heart started shimmying in his chest the way the car did if he drove it over seventy miles per hour. The sweat dripped down his temple and his mouth went dry.

His eye flicked to the bottle in the backseat, full of his magical, calming elixir.

Arriving in front of the house he felt his stomach lurch and he floored the gas, sending up a quick stench of rubber into the air. The house grew smaller in his rear-view mirror.

Not today. Today was not the day. But soon. Soon.

Like Delilah, the swans had also stayed on, two more transient souls making Macaenas their home. Delilah spent her lunch hours tossing bread crumbs to them from beneath the shade of a willow tree. Her days felt strange, empty of Virginia, yet she fell into them with surprising ease. Whatever she had lost had been replaced by something else. Something she couldn't yet name but that settled comfortably around her, steadying her. She had even begun to imagine this place in fall and winter, the way the landscape would change; she pictured herself shoveling the snow from Virginia's walkway, curling on the sofa in a blanket with a cup of hot cocoa watching the leaves slowly give way, the snowfall move in. She began to see a future here, a life beyond the now.

"'There, swan-like, let me sing and die.' Lord Byron..." Harold had a way of appearing out of thin air, catching Delilah off guard. Leaping to her feet she spun toward him, several moments passing before she realized who it was. "Jesus! Harold! Step on a twig or something, will you? My heart can't take it!"

Harold stood quietly, his brow knit, his breath coming sharp and shallow, his lips suddenly moving rapidly in silent repetition. Then in an instant, he turned and ran—across the field, across the road, legs and arms pumping wildly askew. Like a newborn colt, uncoordinated and disconnected, he ran.

200

"Harold!" she called, desperately wanting him to stop, knowing he was already too far away to hear. Her mouth opened and closed without sound. She leaned forward, yearning for motion, wanting to follow him, but her legs remained planted beneath her, unwilling to comply. Her mouth filled with a sour, metallic taste as self-loathing welled within her, a familiar, forgotten feeling.

And then he was gone.

"Let me sing and die."

Through the beating sun, and vision blurred by tears, Harold ran home muttering breathlessly. "...'Thy friends are exaltations, agonies...' William Wordsworth..."

He ran down Main street past the produce market and the familiar stares and shaking heads. He ran to just before Main became Route One, where he turned down the dirt drive leading into the woods. An old sofa sat overturned in the bushes, the bottom ripped out, cushions missing. Up the porch steps of the grey, clapboard house he ran, past the broken lamp, its wires strewn like entrails, down the hallway, his backpack leaving pock marks in the plaster as his body bounced from wall to wall, then he slammed the door to his bedroom before collapsing to the floor in a fresh wash of tears.

His back was sore where the heavy backpack had struck it all the way home, and his mind raced with a mix of feelings he couldn't untangle—anger at Delilah for yelling at him, fear that he would again be alone, pain that he had scared Delilah as he had.

He knew that, like himself, she didn't like to be frightened. And he had done it to her anyway. Even if accidentally.

Delilah was the first real friend he'd had in a long time. Adults, no matter how kind, scared him. He did not trust them.

Delilah understood things about him without him ever having to explain.

But now he might have scared her away. He might have made her so angry that she might not want him any longer.

He rocked back and forth on the floor his arc increasing until his head began to strike the wall beside the bed, "Not again, no, not again, no, no...," he whispered in time with the rhythm. Harder and harder he rocked, and harder his head struck the wall until he heard a far away ringing in his ears that finally drowned out the miserable voices in his mind.

He remained there, pressed against the wall, all afternoon until the ringing in his ears had died down. Then he walked across town and loitered across the street from the hat shop, walking the curb where he'd set his backpack, one foot up on the sidewalk, one in the gutter, up, down, up, down, up, down, thinking about Delilah. "Delilah... Delilah," he sang the name softly to himself, "*Delilah of sunhats and Swans*... Harold Reinman."

All afternoon at work Delilah agonized over Harold, fidgeting with displays, moping behind the counter, hoping she hadn't destroyed what had begun between them. Trust. Like a feral stray, Harold needed coaxing, softness, slow, predictable moves to lure him into closeness and comfort. Now all that may be gone.

When the shop finally closed, Delilah considered making a stop at Harold's house but couldn't decide what to say if she did. The early evening light made her melancholy enough, the way it softened edges and seemed to be coaxing the shadows to rise like the maiden tempting the mythical unicorn.

She didn't want to see Harold's gaze go empty on her, the light around him dim. She didn't want to see those things, knowing she was the cause. So instead she strolled through the beginning shadows toward home.

A short distance behind her, Harold followed—up, down, up down, one sneaker untied, laces flapping, backpack slung over his shoulder.

They would have made it all the way home that way had not Harold, in a fit of playful abandon, kicked an old soda can in the gutter with such force that it hit Delilah on her heel.

Harold froze.

Delilah turned and Harold held his breath, afraid she'd be angry again. But her eyes grew wide and she burst out laughing.

"Nice shot!" she called.

Each stood quietly regarding the other through thinly veiled affection. "Care to walk with me?" Delilah asked him.

Harold considered a moment, then began his loping stroll toward Delilah. He was in no particular hurry, even pausing to retrieve a sole butterfly wing lying on the pavement, the soft black pattern powdering onto his fingertips, so it was a minute or so before he reached her.

They stood a moment, looking at each other, finding that comfortable place together and Delilah sighed. "What are you reading these days?" She reached for the backpack but he pulled away.

"Nothing." It came out flat. Empty.

She understood. They were his. Private. They belonged to him and him alone. He took his boundaries where he could. "Okay." So she resumed walking, Harold falling into step beside her. Those that noticed them along the way wouldn't have seen anything unusual. Only if they had looked hard enough to see who it was, only then would it have mattered. As they neared Virginia's, Delilah glanced at Harold as he walked silently beside her, his head down, his gaze fixed on his sneakers. "So, Harold—how about showing me where you live?"

"You already know."

Delilah stopped, smiling. "What?"

Harold kept walking. "I saw you that day. You came to my house."

"Why didn't you say anything?"

Harold stopped and turned to face her. "I see a lot of things."

Delilah beamed at him. She was growing fond of this boy/man. They shared secrets. Private knowledge that only the initiated are aware of. "I know you do. But why didn't you say anything?"

Harold thought a moment. "You were hiding. Hiding means you don't want to be found." He turned away again and resumed walking but only got a few steps before another thought struck him spinning him toward her. "Did you want to be found?" He feared he might have let her down.

"No. I guess I didn't. I wouldn't have been hiding otherwise."

Harold smiled. "That's what I thought."

It turned out that Harold had an instinct for gardening. In all his years of reading, strange knowledge had become trapped in tiny recesses of his brain. Some of that knowledge came as the occasional, literary quote, some came in practical applications, such as his knack with the roses and soil and fertilizer.

Late in the afternoon, just before evening, Harold took Delilah to the back yard and began pruning Virginia's rose bushes. She followed behind as he finished with that and began fertilizing the herb garden, coaching her on each plant. He showed her how if she rubbed the leaves of one it released the fragrance of chocolate mint.

Amazed at the plants, at Harold, Delilah started to laugh. It startled Harold until she explained she wasn't laughing at him, just at the wonder and fun of the things he seemed to know. Then he laughed too. His shoulders shook, his hair shook, his knees nearly buckled, and he laughed.

Amos had just come out of the shower when he heard that laughter. Moving to his bedroom window he saw Harold and Delilah like any two friends spending a day together. He couldn't hear what they were saying, didn't really care. He was simply fascinated by the fact that they had anything to say to each other at all because, in spite of the evening on the porch, away from Delilah, Harold returned to the reclusive, unreachable, autistic-like state the rest of the town had grown accustomed to.

Only Delilah knew the real truth of it, that Harold protected himself from the pain of his world the only way he knew how. He became invisible. Nothing more, nothing less. He simply withdrew to the point that people stopped noticing him.

Only then was he safe.

And, of course, with her.

The next morning Delilah heard the doorbell ring as she stepped from the shower. Wrapping herself in what was once Virginia's robe, she toweled off her hair and went down to the door.

When she opened it, Harold greeted her from the front porch, a bouquet of wildflowers clutched in his hand.

"Harold! Good morning!" She opened the screen door and stood aside to invite him in.

"Good morning." Harold said as he walked passed, then turned and extended the flowers. "These are for you."

Delilah smiled, closing the door behind her. "Oh, they're beautiful!" She took the flowers from him and headed for the kitchen. "I made some coffee," she called over her shoulder, "do you want some?"

When she didn't get an answer, she turned to find Harold just inside the front door, his lips pursed in confusion.

"Harold? What are you doing? Come on in here."

He lumbered back to the kitchen and sat at the table as Delilah poured them both a cup of coffee.

She sat down, spooned sugar and poured milk into her mug, suddenly aware that Harold sat stiffly across from her. "Have you ever had coffee?"

Harold looked at his mug and shook his head.

"Do you want to try it?"

He shrugged.

Delilah smiled, sifted two spoonfuls of sugar into Harold's coffee and enough milk to turn it pale tan. Then she sat back, picked up her own mug, blew across the surface and took a small sip.

After watching her intently, Harold, in perfect imitation, followed Delilah's every move, finally setting his mug down on the table and smiling.

"Well?" Delilah asked.

"I like it."

"Good."

"Yup. I like coffee."

The next morning he and Delilah met at Amos' counter for breakfast before Delilah went to work.

"Morning!" Amos turned, surprised to find Harold sitting beside Delilah, a broad, close-lipped grin cutting across his face. "Harold! Well now, what a surprise." He looked from one to the other, looking for the punch line, but both sat silent and bemused as the sphinx. "What can I get for you?"

Harold looked to Delilah as she ordered first. "Oh, let's go with a coffee and a muffin. And maybe a little bowl of fruit."

Amos nodded and turned toward Harold. "Harold? How about you? Anything?"

Harold thought a moment, biting his lower lip, then with a deep intake of breath for courage he said, "I'll have the same."

Amos stifled a laugh. "You want coffee? I don't think I've ever seen you drink coffee, Harold."

Millie and Sarah Martinson had come in during the conversation, taking a booth off to the side not quite out of earshot.

Harold glanced quickly at Delilah who nodded encouragement. "I like it." His confidence wavered, uncomfortable with the sudden audience of two behind them.

"Well, okay then." Amos tapped the counter with his finger and then spoke over their heads toward the booth. "You two ladies like some coffee?"

"Yes, thanks, Amos," Millie replied, without ever taking her eyes off the pair at the counter. "You know, Sarah," Millie continued, "I've said it before and I'll say it again, whatever magic that girl has, it sure as hell is working on Harold. It's the damnedest thing."

Sarah glanced quickly over her shoulder where Delilah and Harold were spooning sugar into their coffee."

"Mm. It's nice to see Harold actually reaching out. But I have to admit, it's sort of odd to see, too, you know? I'm so used to him being withdrawn. And what prompted it, anyway? I know for a fact both Virginia and Amos have tried to bring him around for years. They could never do it."

"It's Delilah, dammit. I don't know how or why, but it's her. I wish I knew."

Amos brought over two cups of coffee and set them on the table. "Anything else, ladies?"

"Yes, actually." Millie tore open a package of sweetener. "I'd like some whole wheat toast..." she glanced up at him with a Cheshire cat grin, "and some of whatever it is that makes Delilah—well—Delilah."

Amos smiled and threw a look over his shoulder. Delilah was coaching Harold on adding milk to his coffee. "I'm afraid I don't know what that is. That's Delilah's secret."

Delilah and Harold laughed at something no one else had heard. Or perhaps, something they simply did not know, leaving the elder trio at the table to simply stare—and wonder.

And oddly enough, the strangeness of Harold's transformation, the fact that Delilah seemed so pivotal to its arrival and its remaining, prompted Millie, Amos and others to continue to steer clear, which gave Harold and Delilah room to become true and honest friends.

Over the next week Harold and Delilah were inseparable, and in that time, Harold began to change.

One evening Millie sat outside as Delilah and Harold walked by. "Hey you two..."

Delilah looked up. "Hi, Millie. Beautiful night."

"Sure is. I love when we get a cool spell in the middle of summer's dog days."

Harold rocked quietly back and forth as they talked and then suddenly said, "We're going to the pond."

Millie wasn't sure he was speaking to her until she noticed Delilah smiling at her.

"You are? Well that's a great idea! It's the perfect night for a walk by the pond."

"Yup. Perfect night. 'Nothing is rich but the inexhaustible wealth of nature. She shows us only surfaces, but she is a million fathoms deep.' Ralph Waldo Emerson."

Millie smiled, shook her head, and ran her hands back through her hair. She raised her eyebrows, nearly laughed, sighed instead. "Well, you two have a nice evening."

Delilah prompted Harold to start walking again as she called over her shoulder, "'Night, Millie!"

Then Millie heard Harold, parroting Delilah, "'Night, Millie!"

And Millie was left alone on her swing, full, laughing, happy.

"Delilah," Harold began as he sat on the ground near the pond, "can I ask you a question?"

"Yup." Delilah picked a fat blade of grass, stretched it between her fingers, and blew a long, razzing sound that echoed toward the trees and made Harold laugh.

When the echo died away he continued. "What makes people hurt other people?"

Once again this reportedly simple-minded individual dropped a hefty one in her lap. "I don't know. I wish I did." She glanced up at him and saw his inquisitive gaze trained on her. "I suppose they are unhappy, and they take that unhappiness out on others. Make them hurt so they aren't alone in their pain."

"I knew, you know. The first time I saw you."

"Knew what?"

"That you were like me."

She smiled at him and looked away, shyness bringing a flush to her cheek.

Harold tried to see her face, but a breeze tossed her hair in the way. "You don't believe me."

She tucked her hair behind her ears. "Actually, I do. I have no doubt in my mind that you knew right away."

"I did." In a move that startled them both, Harold placed his hand on hers. It so touched her, carried so much affection and honesty that Delilah fell speechless. Harold gently squeezed her hand as he spoke again, "'The mind is its own place, and in itself can make a heaven of hell, a hell of heaven.' John Milton. Paradise Lost."

Delilah swallowed and squeezed Harold's hand in return. "Thank you."

Harold smiled, rocking gently back and forth. "You're welcome." Although he wasn't entirely sure what for.

They looked at one another then, each gazing directly at the other, and Delilah experienced a sudden, unspoken comprehension. She no longer felt the common companion of a knot in her stomach or an ache in her heart, and looking at Harold, his shoulders relaxed, his hands still, his gaze clear, she was sure he felt the same calm. She became certain at that moment that friendship, in the truest, purest sense, was precisely what they had discovered in one another.

And whether that was by fate or circumstance or sheer luck remained unclear, but the reason was inconsequential to each. For both of them, it simply *was*.

*L*ate one afternoon, after the gardening lesson, Delilah and Harold retreated to the kitchen where Delilah thought she might, finally, try Virginia's muffin recipe. She donned an apron pulled her hair back into a ponytail, and turned on the small radio sitting on the counter. Soft strains of classical music drifted through the kitchen.

Delilah rubbed her hands together then patted Harold on the shoulder. "Well, Harold, I hope you're as good at baking as you are at gardening." She pulled the ingredients out onto the kitchen table.

"Me?" Harold looked terrified as he watched her retrieve the sack of flour, sticks of butter, apples, a bag of sugar, measuring spoons and bowls. "Nuh-uh. Not me. Not me."

"No, huh? Okay, well, then we'll just have to wing it, I guess, because it's my birthday today and I want to celebrate."

213

Harold looked puzzled. "With muffins?"

"Why not?"

Harold thought a moment, then shrugged. "Okay. Happy Birthday!"

"Thank you." Delilah smiled and held out her hand.

Harold approached and allowed Delilah to take his hand in hers, and together they looked over the recipe, Delilah reading the ingredients and Harold locating them on the table.

While Delilah cut apples, Harold measured dry ingredients. As he spooned the powdered sugar, a puff escaped from the box which Harold inhaled and coughed out, sending the measuring cup full of sugar to the floor and Delilah into a fit of laughter she thought would leave her permanently breathless. And when Harold stepped in the spill, tracking powdered footprints all around the kitchen, she laughed even harder. She pretended to perform a soft-shoe in the powder, like she'd seen in old movies, and made faces that sent Harold into whooping, childish giggles.

An hour later there was flour on the table, butter pats on the floor, sugar on their elbows and somehow in their shirt pockets and the two of them sat on kitchen chairs eating slices of tart, green apple. Harold laughed a full, staccato laugh that rang through the kitchen in a way that made the house, itself, sound alive. "I don't think this is how Virginia made them!" he crowed, his speech muffled by a large wedge of apple that slipped out of the corner of his mouth.

"You don't think so?" Delilah laughed. "Yeah, well, I bet she never had as much fun as we just had." She dipped her finger into a pile of powdered sugar and stuck it in her mouth. The powder quickly dissolved on her tongue.

"But we didn't make any muffins," Harold said.

"I don't care. Do you?"

Harold thought a moment, snapshots of the afternoon playing through his head and he smiled. "Nope! I don't care either!" And he didn't. He only knew there was no knot in his stomach and the sound of his own laughter made him happy.

Delilah breathed deeply and relaxed against the chair, enjoying Harold's presence in a house that had threatened to scream of emptiness. And looking in her heart, she realized he was there as well, chasing away shadows with his floppy hair and silly laughter.

She knew it was the first time in forever that they both felt truly at home.

And that evening as Harold drifted to sleep on the couch in the living room, a book open on his chest, Delilah watched him—the way his body fought slumber, jerking and twitching, waking briefly several times before sleep took hold, small whimpers escaping when dreams rolled in. How alone he must be.

How afraid and unsure.

How like her.

The next morning Delilah took the day off work and was just putting cereal on the kitchen table when Harold jolted awake so fiercely that he fell off the living room couch. An unnatural sight in a grown man.

"Oh! Harold!" She tried not to laugh, not wanting to embarrass him. "Are you okay?"

Harold leapt immediately to his feet, eyes darting as he tried to place his surroundings.

"Harold? It's okay. It's Delilah. You're okay." She moved toward him.

Slowly Harold calmed. He glanced at the sofa behind him, the overstuffed cushions still mashed from his body in sleep, at the overturned book on the floor. "I fell asleep." He became shy.

"Yeah. You did." Delilah smiled. He was so simple, so honest, so genuine. So rare.

"I'm sorry." He did not look at her, only prodded the book with his toe.

Delilah laughed, not at him, but at his funny need to offer apologies for things that required none. Something else familiar. "Don't be. I don't mind. C'mon, have some breakfast." She led him toward the table and coaxed him to sit down. "Hope you like Fruit Loops!" She shook the box as she sat down. Her clothes were the same as yesterday. She hadn't slept. New thoughts dogged her throughout the night, happiness being one. And the fear of trusting that happiness.

"I don't know. I've never had them." Harold still seemed to struggle with his shyness. She supposed he wasn't used to waking up somewhere other than his house. It made him nervous.

"Well, then you're in for a treat! It's like dessert for breakfast!" She leaned across the table to pour cereal into his bowl. Suddenly his fingers reached out and brushed along the scar on her wrist.

"Did you hurt yourself?" he asked. "Like me?" He pushed his tousled hair to the side where his own scar hid.

Delilah bit down hard, her lips pressed together, her back muscles tight and sank back into her chair. She couldn't avoid this one. Not with Harold. Not with those huge, dark eyes fixed on her. "Yeah. Yeah, I did."

"Why?"

No one had ever asked, so hearing it now felt like cold water in her face. She nearly forgot how to breathe, and struggled to swallow the rock that materialized in her throat.

Harold's face changed. He dropped his gaze, his features sagging, and took several shallow breaths. He didn't seem to know where to look, perhaps regretting the question. "Mine was because I was bad," he offered.

"What? No, I don't think..."

"Yes. I wasn't a very good boy. I was too loud, and too clumsy. I didn't use my head. I think I do better now, though."

The truth grew too strong for Delilah and she felt the tension in her stomach. The burning behind her eyes. She took Harold's hand in hers. "You aren't bad, Harold. And I'm very sure that you never were. We've both been told a lot of lies, Harold. Lies that hurt."

If Harold heard her he didn't respond. He simply moved his fingers along her scar again and the innocence of it was nearly more than Delilah could take. "Why did you get hurt?" he asked again.

Delilah looked at her wrist, at one of two scars she'd long ignored, and searched for a reason. There were so many. "I was sad. And alone."

Harold nodded. "I get sad. Do you think I'll get hurt like this?"

Good God! How could this half-man know so very much and yet know so little? It was almost impossible to comprehend how all the conflicting parts of him managed to work together well enough for him to function. "No. You won't get hurt like this." She stated it firmly in the hopes that sounding certain would make it so.

"How do you know?"

Delilah looked at him, the answer suddenly as clear as rainwater. "Because you aren't alone, Harold. I'm here." She didn't know if he'd understand what was in her head, but she suddenly felt it was important to try. For both of them. She understood the moment and its importance. *This* was the precipice they must both leap off in order to be free. She had to talk the thought through to find it. Remaining silent would guarantee its loss. "You and I are the same Harold, like you said. We had crappy parents and no childhood but managed to survive anyway. We know the truth about the world and people. And even though it hurts, we're still here." She brushed her fingertips across the scar on his head. She'd never spoken the words, never allowed the thoughts to solidify in such a way, afraid they would shatter her. Instead, they seemed to give her strength.

Harold looked up at her, full of an understanding of her meaning, if not all of the words. "Then that means you aren't alone, either. Right?" He covered one of her scars with his palm.

For a moment Delilah became lost. A thought struggled to form in her mind and she tried to relax and allow it to step forward. Something simple was out of place, or needed correcting. Then, as Harold withdrew his hand and returned to his dry Fruit Loops, and as Delilah stared at the scars on her wrists, in that instant, it came clear.

"No one need feel alone in this world, child," Virginia's words echoed back to her, *"There's always someone who cares."*

Something both of them just proved.

The answer was so simple.

"Harold..." She paused, waiting for him to look up at her, "why don't you come live here?"

Harold thought a moment, picturing his home, imagined leaving it and how that would feel. His brow furrowed, then his eyes lit up like fireworks and he smiled. "Here, instead of alone?"

"Yup."

"Will I have to sleep on the couch?"

Delilah laughed. "No! You'll get your own room."

"Because we're friends," Harold said.

"You bet," Delilah replied, "the best."

Harold thought a moment more then added, "No bad dreams here."

"Nope," agreed Delilah. "Not anymore."

And for the first time in her life Delilah found herself truly looking forward, toward the future—her future.

She remembered how last year, six months after her eighteenth birthday she began spending afternoons at the library poring over maps of the country. She traced red roads and yellow highways with her finger, whispering the names of small, finely-printed towns to see how they sounded. She went to the bus station and stared at the departure board. She bought a ticket, valid for six months from date of purchase. She wrote the town names on the bus route on a piece of paper and slept with them under her pillow. And she planned. Soon. Soon she would leave this life and find another. One with softness and light. One as far away from this nightmare as she could find.

Now it seemed that that life had found her. In this time, this boy-man, this house. She was finally, she thought, home.

The next morning Delilah took the day off work and was just putting cereal on the kitchen table when Harold jolted awake so fiercely that he fell off the living room couch. An unnatural sight in a grown man.

"Oh! Harold!" She tried not to laugh, not wanting to embarrass him. "Are you okay?"

Harold leapt immediately to his feet, eyes darting as he tried to place his surroundings.

"Harold? It's okay. It's Delilah. You're okay." She moved toward him.

Slowly Harold calmed. He glanced at the sofa behind him, the overstuffed cushions still mashed from his body in sleep, at the overturned book on the floor. "I fell asleep." He became shy.

"Yeah. You did." Delilah smiled. He was so simple, so honest, so genuine. So rare.

"I'm sorry." He did not look at her, only prodded the book with his toe.

Delilah laughed, not at him, but at his funny need to offer apologies for things that required none. Something else familiar. "Don't be. I don't mind. C'mon, have some breakfast." She led him toward the table and coaxed him to sit down. "Hope you like Fruit Loops!" She shook the box as she sat down. Her clothes were the same as yesterday. She hadn't slept. New thoughts dogged her throughout the night, happiness being one. And the fear of trusting that happiness.

"I don't know. I've never had them." Harold still seemed to struggle with his shyness. She supposed he wasn't used to waking up somewhere other than his house. It made him nervous.

"Well, then you're in for a treat! It's like dessert for breakfast!" She leaned across the table to pour cereal into his bowl. Suddenly his fingers reached out and brushed along the scar on her wrist.

"Did you hurt yourself?" he asked. "Like me?" He pushed his tousled hair to the side where his own scar hid.

Delilah bit down hard, her lips pressed together, her back muscles tight and sank back into her chair. She couldn't avoid this one. Not with Harold. Not with those huge, dark eyes fixed on her. "Yeah. Yeah, I did."

"Why?"

No one had ever asked, so hearing it now felt like cold water in her face. She nearly forgot how to breathe, and struggled to swallow the rock that materialized in her throat.

Harold's face changed. He dropped his gaze, his features sagging, and took several shallow breaths. He didn't seem to know where to look, perhaps regretting the question. "Mine was because I was bad," he offered.

"What? No, I don't think..."

"Yes. I wasn't a very good boy. I was too loud, and too clumsy. I didn't use my head. I think I do better now, though."

The truth grew too strong for Delilah and she felt the tension in her stomach. The burning behind her eyes. She took Harold's hand in hers. "You aren't bad, Harold. And I'm very sure that you never were. We've both been told a lot of lies, Harold. Lies that hurt."

If Harold heard her he didn't respond. He simply moved his fingers along her scar again and the innocence of it was nearly more than Delilah could take. "Why did you get hurt?" he asked again.

Delilah looked at her wrist, at one of two scars she'd long ignored, and searched for a reason. There were so many. "I was sad. And alone."

Harold nodded. "I get sad. Do you think I'll get hurt like this?"

Good God! How could this half-man know so very much and yet know so little? It was almost impossible to comprehend how all the conflicting parts of him managed to work together well enough for him to function. "No. You won't get hurt like this." She stated it firmly in the hopes that sounding certain would make it so.

"How do you know?"

Delilah looked at him, the answer suddenly as clear as rainwater. "Because you aren't alone, Harold. I'm here." She didn't know if he'd understand what was in her head, but she suddenly felt it was important to try. For both of them. She understood the moment and its importance. *This* was the precipice they must both leap off in order to be free. She had to talk the thought through to find it. Remaining silent would guarantee its loss. "You and I are the same Harold, like you said. We had crappy parents and no childhood but managed to survive anyway. We know the truth about the world and people. And even though it hurts, we're still here." She brushed her fingertips across the scar on his head. She'd never spoken the words, never allowed the thoughts to solidify in such a way, afraid they would shatter her. Instead, they seemed to give her strength.

Harold looked up at her, full of an understanding of her meaning, if not all of the words. "Then that means you aren't alone, either. Right?" He covered one of her scars with his palm.

For a moment Delilah became lost. A thought struggled to form in her mind and she tried to relax and allow it to step forward. Something simple was out of place, or needed correcting. Then, as Harold withdrew his hand and returned to his dry Fruit Loops, and as Delilah stared at the scars on her wrists, in that instant, it came clear.

"No one need feel alone in this world, child," Virginia's words echoed back to her, *"There's always someone who cares."*

223

Something both of them just proved.

The answer was so simple.

"Harold..." She paused, waiting for him to look up at her, "why don't you come live here?"

Harold thought a moment, picturing his home, imagined leaving it and how that would feel. His brow furrowed, then his eyes lit up like fireworks and he smiled. "Here, instead of alone?"

"Yup."

"Will I have to sleep on the couch?"

Delilah laughed. "No! You'll get your own room."

"Because we're friends," Harold said.

"You bet," Delilah replied, "the best."

Harold thought a moment more then added, "No bad dreams here."

"Nope," agreed Delilah. "Not anymore."

And for the first time in her life Delilah found herself truly looking forward, toward the future—her future.

She remembered how last year, six months after her eighteenth birthday she began spending afternoons at the library poring over maps of the country. She traced red roads and yellow highways with her finger, whispering the names of small, finely-printed towns to see how they sounded. She went to the bus station and stared at the departure board. She bought a ticket, valid for six months from date of purchase. She wrote the town names on the bus route on a piece of paper and slept with them under her pillow. And she planned. Soon. Soon she would leave this life and find another.

One with softness and light. One as far away from this nightmare as she could find.

Now it seemed that that life had found her. In this time, this boy-man, this house. She was finally, she thought, home.

*T*he morning after the attempt at muffins, the first day of her nineteenth year, Delilah woke early, surprised to realize she slept soundly and peacefully for the first time in her life.

She showered, put on a pale blue sundress, then, her hair still damp and hanging down her back, she went to the kitchen to make coffee.

Maybe it was the good night's sleep, maybe she just never saw it before, but it seemed the kitchen was bursting with morning sunshine. Light gleamed off the cabinet handles and reflected off the floor tiles. It was as though the curtains had been opened for the first time, flooding the room with bright warmth.

She whistled to herself as she went about the business of filling the coffee maker. At first it was unconscious, but eventually she became aware of a tune. A familiar one. After a moment she placed it as being the same tune Virginia had always hummed during her morning routine. The one Delilah heard as she leaned on the windowsill of her bedroom window. She smiled, finally remembering her friend with happiness, rather than heartache.

While the coffee brewed she went back upstairs and began moving her things into Virginia's old room. She moved her clothes into Virginia's closet and dresser, put her shoes under the bed, her brush and make-up on the vanity. All the while she felt full, bubbly, real contentment settling in around her. She opened the windows to the morning air, filling the rooms with a sweet, dewy scent. Then she changed the sheets in her old room, put some of Virginia's books on the dresser, fluffed the pillows and made the room ready for Harold. She looked forward to him living there, both of them ready to find a way to live *in* life, rather than just passing through it. She'd lived that way long enough. Once it was out of need, then habit; there was no excuse any longer.

Once the bedrooms were ready, she returned to the kitchen and poured a cup of coffee. Leaning against the counter in a slant of sun she picked up the phone and called Amos.

"Hello?"

"Hi, it's Delilah."

"Hi... you've never called me on the phone before, it's odd."

Delilah set her coffee on the table and turned to face the window over the sink. She breathed in the sweet smell of dew on the grass. "Yeah, well, there's a first time for everything."

"Are you okay?"

"Fine. I'm fine, you old worry-wart. I need to borrow you and your truck this afternoon."

"Mind if I ask what for?"

"Nope."

Silence fell across the line until Amos snorted a laugh. "Goddammit. One of these days I'll learn."

Delilah laughed and sat in a chair at the table. "No you won't. And because of that I'll take pity and tell you without any further torture."

"Oh, well, how kind of you."

"I need you to help me move Harold out of his house and into here."

Again the line fell silent, although Delilah could hear Amos breathing. She imagined him pacing back and forth, hand massaging the back of his neck. "Amos?"

"Yeah, I'm here. Harold is moving in with you?"

"Well, into this house, yes. I spoke with him about it last night. It's perfect, don't you think?"

Amos sighed and laughed again. "I'll be goddamned."

"So will you help?"

"Of course I'll help. Shit! This is the best damned thing I've heard in a while. Shit." He paused. "Delilah..."

"What?"

Amos' voice grew small. "Nothing."

Delilah rose and returned to the kitchen window. She leaned on the counter looking toward Amos' house. "Amos, what?"

Amos breathed deeply twice and Delilah was certain he was rubbing his eyes. "I just... you're a good person, Delilah. I've never said that to you, but I've always thought it. You are a truly special human being."

Now it was Delilah who fell silent, caught off guard by Amos' sudden candor. But then she heard him, truly heard the words, and the sound buoyed her, warmed her. She smiled. "Ditto, Amos. I'll come by in a couple of hours."

"See you then."

Delilah went to Amos' just before noon, and together they drove to Harold's house.

Harold sat on the front porch surrounded by two suitcases, his backpack, several boxes, and a rocking chair Amos recognized as being from the living room.

Delilah jumped out of the truck as it pulled to a stop. "Harold! Hey! How long have you been sitting out here?"

Harold shrugged and glanced to Amos.

Amos smiled. "Hi. Delilah asked me to help you two move your stuff. I think it's great that you are going to live there."

Harold nodded but appeared distressed, his brow wrinkled, his hands clenched.

Amos stood back as Delilah walked up to the porch. "What is it, Harold?"

Harold twisted a strand of hair and looked at her. "Amos brings me peanut butter."

Amos and Delilah exchanged a confused look, then suddenly Amos figured it out. "Do you think I won't do that anymore?"

Harold scratched his ear and nodded. "I won't live here anymore, so you won't come."

Amos smiled. "How about if I bring you peanut butter at Virginia's?"

Harold paused, his eyes darting back and forth as his brain strung the thoughts together. He looked up to Amos. "Bring me peanut butter to my new home?"

"Yup. I can do that."

Harold smiled and looked at Delilah, who nodded.

"Okay!" Harold clapped his hands and picked up his backpack. Then he jumped off the porch, climbed into the truck, and sitting in the middle of the seat he proclaimed, "'So here I sit in the early candle-light of old age — I and my book — casting backward glances over our travel'd road.' Walt Whitman."

Once back at Virginia's house, Amos was unloading the last box of Harold's belongings as Millie drove by. She slowed, pulling up alongside him.

"Afternoon, Amos."

Amos smiled. "How are you?"

Millie glanced to the front porch where Delilah and Harold stood talking. "What's going on?"

Amos followed Millie's gaze then turned back to her, resting the box on the edge of the truck bed. He rubbed his neck, then his chin. "Well, Harold is moving in here."

Millie paused and Amos watched her absorb the news. "Really!" she finally exclaimed. "I'll be a son of a bitch!" She looked again at the two on the porch and her demeanor calmed, softened, quieted. "Well," she continued, "good for Harold. He's waited a long time for a home and a family."

Amos glanced over his shoulder. "Yup. He has. So has Delilah."

Millie smiled. "Tell them I said hello, will you?"

"I sure will."

They paused a moment, just looking at one another. Finally, Millie said, "It's kind of miraculous, isn't it? Those two?"

Amos thought for a second. "Actually, I think that's how it's supposed to be."

The scream that woke Delilah sent her leaping from bed before she was fully awake or aware. She stood in the darkness, disoriented, looking for the door in the wrong place, stubbing her toe on the bureau. Then she remembered she was in Virginia's old room. And the screams came from Harold.

She ran across the hall and found Harold turning slow circles near the bed in the glow of a nightlight. He breathed soft whimpers as he turned, his arms wrapped tightly around himself.

"Harold?" Delilah whispered. "It's okay. It's Delilah. You're okay."

At the sound of her voice Harold quieted. "Delilah?" he asked.

"Yeah. C'mon." She coaxed him back into bed and pulled the sheet up around him. "You remember where you are?"

Harold looked around the room. "Virginia's house. I remember now." He looked at Delilah, his eyes as wide as a child's. "I was lost. I woke up and nothing was right."

Delilah perched on the edge of the bed and took his hand. "I know. But you're okay. This is your home now. Your room. You're safe here." She felt him relax as she stroked his arm.

"Safe," Harold repeated, his eyes beginning to close.

Delilah remained until Harold's breathing slowed and deepened in sleep. Then, leaving the door to both their rooms open, she climbed back into her own bed and slowly drifted off.

The next morning Delilah woke and found Harold in her doorway dressed in jeans and a t-shirt, hair still mashed from sleep.

"Harold?" she asked, concerned he'd had another nightmare.

"I keep thinking about Fruit Loops." Harold replied.

Delilah laughed and pushed herself up, wiping the sleep from her eyes. "Fruit Loops, huh? Well, we can do that."

In the kitchen they sat eating cereal, the morning sun slightly hidden behind high, wispy clouds. Delilah already liked having Harold there. Even if they just sat quietly together, the silence wasn't as loud. The house wasn't as empty.

"Harold..." Delilah began, "I have to go to work today. Will you be okay here?"

Harold chewed his Fruit Loops and drank some orange juice. "What about coffee at Amos'?"

"We can go have coffee first."

"Then I have to go to the library."

"Okay. Sounds like we have a plan!" Delilah finished her cereal. "I'm going to get dressed and then we'll go. Okay?"

Harold looked up at her and smiled. "Okay."

When Delilah came home that evening she was surprised that Harold wasn't there. She still wasn't completely sure how his brain was wired, and she hoped he remembered not to go to his old house. Then she thought he might be with Amos, remembered Harold had been on his own for a long while, and was capable of fending for himself. It was hard, though, feeling responsible for someone else. *Wanting* to be responsible. Caring. Caring was hard.

In the kitchen, she opened the refrigerator and stared at the contents hoping something would strike her as an idea for dinner. She needed to pick some things up at Amos'. She thought she might do that tomorrow on her way home.

A few moments later she heard a knock at the door. She walked down the hall as she made a mental shopping list for the next day, and upon opening the door she found Harold standing on the porch. His finger twirled the curls in his hair, an action she now understood signaled uncertainty.

"Hey! What's up? Did you forget your key?" She stood aside to let Harold in.

"No." Reaching into his pocket, he withdrew the house key and showed it to her.

"Oh. Well, you know you don't have to knock. You live here. Just use the key and come on in!"

Harold pursed his lips and scratched his head. He stared at his sneakers. "I guess I forgot."

"That's okay. Like I said, it might take some time to get used to. Okay?"

"Okay."

Delilah smiled. She hugged him, feeling his body tense for just a moment before giving into it. "Don't worry. Just give it some time."

"'Time dissipates to shining ether the solid angularity of facts.' Ralph Waldo Emerson."

She squeezed him tighter, liking the feel of it, human contact. "Whatever you say, Harold."

Jack sat at a bar not far from his motel trying to figure out where the past week and a half had gone. He should have been halfway home by now with all of this settled and done. With life back to some semblance of normal.

He laughed, which came out more like a sputter and ordered another scotch. Double. No ice. *"Normal?"* he thought. He couldn't recall what that looked like. Not for certain. Then again, he couldn't recall the color of his socks, either.

The thing that had bothered him most all along is how everyone seemed to find it so difficult to comprehend him. He's a pretty straight forward guy. He didn't ask for much—just a little loyalty. He just didn't want to be alone. Why was that so bad? He just wanted those he loved to love him back.

Shaking his head he cursed the selfishness of others, drained his glass, and ordered another.

"Kinda early to be going at it, isn't it?" the bartender asked.

Jack clenched his jaw and looked up at the older man, at his balding head and small, dark eyes. "Not for me. I think better with a drink in my hand. And I've got a lot to think about."

"Well, then let me order you something to eat. On the house..."

"I'm not hungry." Here it comes. If he wanted something to eat, he'd ask for it. Was he speaking Chinese? Did he somehow fail to make his request clear? Thinking perhaps he hadn't, he tried again. "I am thirsty, however. So how about filling this glass for me? Just like the last time." He smiled, though he didn't mean it.

The bartender hesitated. Just a fraction of a pause. But Jack saw it. It registered somewhere in the growing fog around his brain, and the adrenaline it fired up mixed with the alcohol in a crescendoing wave. "You know, I can't understand why my requests always seem so goddamn difficult for people to understand." He rose unsteadily from his seat, glassy-eyed, full of irate menace that radiated strongly enough to make the bartender step back. "Am I unclear? Too vague? Do I make unreasonable demands?" He was no longer talking about the drink, things bleeding and bending together in

235

his mind so he could no longer recall where the anger began. It simply was.

He grabbed the glass, his knuckles white. "Why is it so fucking impossible to get what I want!" He hurled the glass across the bar smashing it against the cash register not three inches from the bartender's shoulder. "Fuck you," Jack muttered to no one as he stumbled from the bar. "Fuck everybody."

After fumbling with his keys, dropping them twice and cracking his head on the side mirror when retrieving them, Jack finally managed to open the car door and slip inside.

His hands shook with rage as tears of frustration pooled in his eyes. He struck the steering wheel with both fists and yelled, "Fuck you all!" Then leaning his head back against the seat, tired of sadness and hurt, he made a decision.

He'd wasted enough time. If she was so hell bent on leaving him alone, if she didn't care that he loved her more than anything in the world, fine. He didn't need her, or anyone else.

He'd let her go.

But he'd make sure she never forgot him either.

Jamming the car into gear, he peeled out of the parking lot and headed back toward the motel to pack his things. Soon he'd be on his way home, and just having made the decision, he felt clearer than he had in a long, long time.

It was almost over.

The following afternoon Delilah found Harold sitting outside Amos' store when she came by for lunch. She watched him for a moment as he read his book, feet tapping at the dirt as though they had a mind of their own.

She felt it in her stomach first, that strange lurch that moved up into her chest and she realized how much she cared for him. His gentle spirit, his exuberance when he allowed himself to feel it. She felt as safe with him as he felt with her. She wasn't sure what it was she felt for him, knew it must be some form of love, but she had felt all the variations so little in her life she didn't know quite where this feeling fit.

"Hi, Delilah." He caught her deep in thought.

"Hey." She smiled and motioned toward the door. "Want to have some lunch?" Again the word love popped into her head and she started contemplating allowing herself to really feel it. To discover what kind of love it was. At the very least it was the love for a true friend. Perhaps even for family. Perhaps.

"Okay." Harold rose from his seat and stuffed his book into his backpack.

Inside they took their usual seat at the counter as Amos stepped out of the back office.

"Hey there!" Amos called to them.

"Afternoon..." Delilah started to answer.

"We're hungry!" Harold interjected.

"Well, I'd say you're in the right place. What can I get you?"

Harold drummed his fingers on the counter then looked up at Amos. "Hamburger. I want a hamburger. But no stuff on it. Just plain."

"Okay. And Delilah?"

"Just a tuna sandwich, on rye, please."

"You got it." Amos put the order in then returned to the counter. "So, how are you two doing? Adjusting to the living arrangements?"

Delilah glanced at Harold who was playing with the salt and pepper shakers. "We're doing okay. Harold just has to remember to use his key instead of knocking." She placed her hand over his.

"I have the key." Harold tapped his front pocket.

Amos smiled. "Man. I'll never know just how you did it, Delilah."

"What?"

Amos nodded to Harold.

"Oh. I don't really do much more than listen. But I guess it's that like attracts like. You know?"

"I suppose I do." Amos rubbed his chin. "Hey, I've been thinking, why don't you two come have dinner at my place?"

"Feeling a sudden need to be social?" Delilah asked, smiling.

"As a matter of fact, yes. Do you take issue with that?" Amos folded his arms and cocked his eyebrow at her.

"Nope. I think it's about time." She turned to Harold. "What do you think, Harold? Do you want to go eat dinner at Amos' house tonight?"

Harold thought a moment. "Can we have peanut butter?"

Delilah and Amos exchanged a quick glance, then Amos answered. "Well, sure. I hadn't thought about it, but why not?"

Harold smiled and jiggled his legs, signaling his consent.

Delilah said, "Well, I guess we'll call you when I get home from work."

"Great. I'll have all the peanut butter you can eat."

Harold wanted to stay at Amos' after dinner.

Amos sat beside him on the couch. "Is everything okay? Do you need something?"

Harold was quiet a moment, his fingers tapping his knees. "I just want to visit. I like you."

Amos opened and closed his mouth without uttering a word, so Delilah spoke up. "No problem Harold. You have fun and I'll see you later."

Amos walked Delilah to the door where she glanced once at Harold as he sat on the couch. "He seems happy, doesn't he?" she asked Amos.

Amos followed her gaze then turned back to her. "Happiest I've ever seen him."

"Good. I'm glad.

"What about you?" he asked her. "Are you happy?"

She looked at him and thought a moment. "As a matter of fact, yes. I am."

"Good." Amos said, "I'm glad." And he held out his arms for an embrace, not thinking until it was too late that he'd never done so before. But Delilah surprised him by stepping into it, allowing herself to be enfolded.

"Thank you, Amos."

"For what?"

"For being who you are." Stepping back, she stood on her toes and kissed him on the cheek. Then she looked to Harold. "See you later!"

"Okay," Harold replied.

Back at home Delilah closed the door behind her and stood a moment in the easy silence. She'd grown comfortable with the sense of Virginia that would forever be part of the house, had come to love the easy ebb and flow of the days, the way the nights descended on the town like a protective covering, shielding all who lived there through another turn of darkness. Yes. This could be home.

She looked around the living room—at the wingback chair, the fireplace, the sofa all wrinkled and baggy and comfortable. She saw herself there years down the line, becoming the woman she thought Virginia would be proud of—tender, solid, wise.

In the kitchen she boiled water and made tea, then curled up on the couch in the quiet living room.

For a moment she wished for a different past, a childhood in a home like this one with a family like Amos and Virginia and Harold. But then maybe she never would have found this town, these people, and she couldn't imagine not having them in her life.

So maybe, even though it was bad, maybe her past was a good one simply for the reason that it led her here.

There was a knock at the door. Kind of a knock. Two short, sharp raps. Perhaps it was Amos, though he usually knocked in three or four soft touches of knuckle against wood. Then she laughed, realizing it must be Harold, still not used to calling this house his home.

"Harold..." Opening the door, she had no time to see anything more than a looming shadow and catch a stale, familiar, sour odor before a stinging blow from Jack Gruffen caught her across the bridge of her nose, sending her sprawling backward. In that split second, a rent in time caused two worlds to ferociously collide, bringing Delilah back to a self she'd been trying to leave behind.

As Jack stepped through the door, Delilah tried to orient herself, hopelessly, blindly flailing her arms and feet—movement painfully natural to her. But he grabbed a fistful of her hair to pull her to her feet. Through gritted teeth, and with a stale, nauseating breath he hissed, "I told you I'd find you." The monster voice of her childhood. He backhanded her across the right cheek, slamming her against the stairs like nothing more than a straw scarecrow, knocking the wind from her.

Daddy was home.

She could taste the blood from her nose in the back of her throat, a familiar, metallic taste of home and family; her right eye had already begun to swell shut, and her lungs burned—rapiers cutting through bruised flesh. She fought to relax the spasm that prevented her from taking in a breath. In less than a moment, the old became the norm again, and the terror churned the bile in her stomach.

In a momentary pause in her father's assault, she caught her breath and struggled to pull herself up the stairs. But her hand slipped and her elbow crashed against the corner of the stair. She heard a sharp crack and felt the pain shoot up into her shoulder.

"Go ahead and scream again," he spat. "I'll fix it so you never utter another sound. You're just like your mother."

Had she screamed? She thought she had heard the swans. But they were mute. Weren't they?

His fist connected again, this time splitting her lip. Her head struck the railing, and she collapsed on the steps a second time. She began to black out, knowing this was the end, and she waited for the final blow that would send her into darkness, setting her, finally, free. From the pain. The past. This life. She held her breath in anticipation. *Go ahead,* she thought.

But the blow never came.

Instead, far down the tunnel of her ebbing awareness, she heard another scream—neither her own, nor the swans—and she sensed the bulky weight of her father falling to the floor. She fought for consciousness, pushing through the fog of pain and fear as she pulled herself up against the wall along the stairs, ignoring the flash of agony through her ribs and the explosion of lights and pain in her brain.

She saw Harold towering over the crumpled figure of Jack, the man she prayed she'd never see again, the man from whom she fled and had begun to believe she'd left in a past far, far behind her. And as he tried to push to his feet, Harold's backpack arced through the air, a shadowed blur, and smashed against Jack's skull, which snapped backward sending him to the floor again. Delilah heard unsettling, inhuman sounds from Harold—wild sounds of pain, rage, anguish. She struggled to call to him, "Harold! Stop!"

But Harold was beyond reach. Even for her. His lips mumbled, almost soundlessly, "'He who shall hurt the little wren/Shall never be belov'd by men.' William Blake," as his boot found Jack's ribcage again and again and again, bones snapping, Jack already still, and just when Delilah could stand it no longer Harold cocked his leg back...

"Harold!"

... and sent the toe of his shoe squarely into the bridge of her father's nose.

"Stop!" It was Amos in the doorway. He tackled Harold who, amazingly, went instantly limp at his touch.

Amos stood a moment, his arms gripping Harold until he felt certain the fight was gone from the young man. Then Amos left him wavering in the doorway like a sapling in the wind, and stepping over the lifeless man on the floor, a man he struggled a moment to recognize, went to Delilah. At the base of the stairs, she sat slumped, shaking and bloody. Amos fought his own shock at the sight of this familiar face nearly unrecognizable.

He glanced back again to the man lying dead on the floor, and to Harold who stood glazed and frozen in the doorway.

Stepping into the living room, he quickly called 911, explained the situation, then turned back to Delilah.

"Jesus, Delilah." He moved her carefully, lifting her in his arms. The last time he carried anyone like this—cradled—it had been Ellen. Now the truth came clear; she was so light, so frail, her body real and damaged—earthly. Nothing miraculous. Just a girl.

"He's dead, isn't he?" She could barely speak through her swollen lip, a jaw visibly bruised, possibly broken, and Amos felt the rage Harold must have felt moments before. Murderous. And then came the sadness. The heartbreak.

As Amos carried her through the door, Delilah saw Harold, bewildered and lost. "Go, Harold."

Amos tried to interrupt. "Delilah..."

"Harold..." She touched his arm, forcing him to see her. "Go. Now."

His eyes darkened as he spun, backpack still in hand, and ran into the woods just as two police cars pulled around the corner. One of them spotted Harold as he disappeared into the woods and followed on foot.

The ambulance arrived as Amos eased quickly down the steps. Delilah winced, took a sharp intake of air, and slipped into unconsciousness.

As Amos rode with Delilah to the hospital, Harold ran toward his house. Voices flooded his brain, screams and insults, painful words followed by painful blows. He saw himself standing in the doorway to the cellar as a boy, his mother, drunk and wild, lunging at him with her fists raised, him stepping backward and falling... falling... then blackness.

At the old house, he stood a moment, his hands shaking, his breath coming in quick rasps. The voices in his head were a blur. He only felt rage and a need to destroy the ghosts that haunted him. Inside him was nothing. He was hollow. Inside the house was his mother. He almost thought he could hear her ranting from room to room, meaningless words strung together in a fit of insane fury. Running in the back door, he dumped out the kitchen drawer and took a pack of matches.

Back outside he lit a match, watching the flame flare up, then dropped it to the dried grass of the yard. Walking to the other corner he did the same, then hid in a stand of bushes a short distance away, watching the flames leap from the dried grass to the house itself. The walls charred, turning black from smoke before catching fire, the heat rising quickly as the inferno slid across the roof, hungry flames sending up thick, acrid clouds of black, billowing smoke filled with tiny sparks flaring off and drifting back down.

The officer who had chased him through the woods arrived just as the flames snaked around the sides of the building, and he momentarily forgot the pursuit to call in the fire. His forgetting allowed Harold to remain a while longer, to witness the result of longstanding horror, to feel the singe of it as the fire grew hungrier still, reaching now for nearby trees. The old house succumbed quickly, the mounting heat nearly evaporating Harold's tears before they fell from his eyes.

He whispered to the flames, and the ghosts they consumed, "'I'll be judge, I'll be jury, said the cunning old Fury; I'll try the whole cause, and condemn you to death.' Alice's Adventures in Wonderland.

Amos followed behind the medics as they carried Delilah into the hospital—the first time he'd set foot inside since Ellen's death. He stayed with her through the exam and her admittance, waiting quietly at her bedside.

He stared helplessly at Delilah's sedated, sleeping body. His breath caught a sharp edge in his chest at the sight of her swollen, stitched lip, the angry, dark bruise on her cheek, her left eye swollen almost shut, and a small, stitched gash by her brow.

He bit back angry tears as the fingers that softly held her right hand traced the scar line on her wrist. The other was hidden beneath a cast to her shoulder.

So much can come so clear so suddenly.

A nurse came in to check on Delilah. She moved quietly through her routine, unobtrusive as a gentle breeze. Suddenly Amos became aware of sirens outside.

"What's going on?" He nodded toward the window.

"Oh, I heard the Reinman house is on fire."

"Oh my god."

"As far as I know there wasn't anyone inside it. But the house is nearly gone." The nurse slipped out the door.

"Oh my God." Amos feared for Harold. But if he was in the house, there was nothing he could do, and if not, he didn't know where the boy could be. But he knew where Delilah was, so that's where he stayed.

He moved to the window, and spotted small wisps of smoke billow up over the treetops in the twilight. Harold. What had he done?

Amid the screeching sound of fire trucks and the sight of the tell-tale smoke dissipating into the dense cobalt sky, Amos stood in the hospital room of an unfathomable young girl whose broken body housed a seemingly invincible spirit, and felt something crack within him. A nearly audible snap set free more sadness and rage than he knew he held, and although he could feel the tears inside, they wouldn't come. Instead the rage just rattled his strong body like a blade of grass in a tempest. He collapsed into the bedside chair, curling himself toward his lap, his head cradled in his hands. With every passing day, understanding seemed to grow more and more elusive. He wanted to believe there was some greater purpose, some ultimate reason for the string of losses that had upset his life and the lives of those near him, but there didn't seem to be any. Just a random strand of unfortunate occurrences.

He plugged his ears against the sirens, listening instead to the amplified sound of his own breathing in his head, the way it sounded almost like a respirator, and for the first time in his life he felt himself wish for death. For an end. He could take no more pain.

The quiet nurse slipped soundlessly toward him. "Mr. Harrison, there's a police officer here to see you." When he didn't respond she walked over to him, tapped him on the shoulder and repeated herself.

Amos shook his head and the nurse left him alone to collect himself. It took five slow, deep breaths to calm his breathing and steady his trembling, then, after splashing some cold water on his face, he readied himself and reached for the door.

On his way out Delilah stirred awake.

"Harold..." she whispered.

He moved to her, "Everything's fine, Delilah. Rest." He stroked her hand briefly, steeling himself against her inquiry and his lie, and quietly left the room.

The hallway smelled flat and pungent, sourness scrubbed clean but not gone, leaving a mix of aromas that was slightly nauseating.

At the other end of the hall stood the nurses desk, elevators on either side of it, and a waiting area a few steps further on the left. Sergeant Tilton sat on the chairs there, waiting.

"Sergeant Tilton..." Amos said as he approached.

The Sergeant stood, shook Amos' hand and motioned for him to take a seat.

"Mr. Harrison, about Delilah..."

Amos cut him off, "Yeah, I know. You need to speak with her, but..."

"No, I know. She's not up to that just yet. I know that. I was actually wondering what *you* could tell me. Where is she from? Family? That sort of thing."

"Delilah has always kept pretty quiet about herself." No wonder.

"But she *has* been living next door to you for several months. You and she have become quite close, yes?"

"The woodchucks live next door too, but I don't know anything about them either."

Sergeant Tilton sighed and lowered his gaze. "Mr. Harrison..."

"I'm sorry. I'm sorry." Amos rubbed his eyes. "The fact is, I know nothing about her. Nobody does." And yet, he knew all he needed to. All that mattered.

"I see. And the man?" Sergeant Tilton glanced at his notebook. "Jack Gruffen?"

"I don't know... I..." Suddenly the memory spilled forward making Amos sick to his stomach. "Mr. Harrison?"

Amos pressed his palms to his forehead. "Oh God."

"What is it?"

"He came into the store recently. 'Seeing this part of the country,' he said. And me and my blithering mouth led him right to her. Son of a bitch."

Sergeant Tilton jotted down notes. "So you spoke with him?"

Amos looked at his hands while he spoke, all the while replaying the scene in his head. "Only briefly. Friendly banter." He looked up at Sergeant Tilton. "I didn't know."

Again Sergeant Tilton wrote in his notebook, shaking his head understandingly.

"Goddamnit!" Amos choked.

Sergeant Tilton paused in his writing. "Mr. Harrison, there's no way you *could* have known. Nothing you could have done."

Amos glanced up. "Is he dead?"

"Yes, he is."

"Good." A moment passed while Amos struggled to pull himself out of his self-beratement, "What about Harold?"

"Oh, well, we haven't found him yet. But his house..."

"Yeah. I heard." Amos laughed. He didn't mean to. It wasn't what he felt. But he laughed—a short, abrupt burst of sound.

"Not that we hope to get much from him when we do find him."

"I don't know. Delilah seemed to get quite a lot from him."

"Really?" Sergeant Tilton rose from his chair. "Well, that's good to know. And we'd appreciate it if..."

"I know. If I think of anything else, I'll call."

"Thank you. And I assume you'll be caring for her?"

Amos paused, not considering until this moment that he felt he'd always been doing just that. Or maybe it had been her caring for him. "Yes, sir, I will." He rose and shook Sergeant Tilton's hand, still reeling from the memory of Jack Gruffen in his store. Buying razors. Seeing the country. Looking for a room.

Looking for Delilah.

$\mathcal{T}$he first night at the hospital seemed endless to Amos.

Exhausted, and sitting at Delilah's bedside staring at the painful-looking tubes drip, drip, dripping sustenance and life directly into her veins, remembering the same scenario with Ellen, he thought, *This isn't how it's supposed to go.* Everyone on the planet had an image of how life would unfold, and while there were inevitable disappointments for all, his life had strayed so far from what he'd foreseen that it almost seemed a farce. This wasn't his life, it was some dramatic interpretation of something else and soon the lights would come up, the curtain would fall, and he would walk back out into reality. Throughout the night Delilah tossed and mumbled, her face contorting in pain, small gasps of fear escaping her lips, as nightmares plagued her in spite of the heavy sedatives they had fed her. Every time she flinched or moaned Amos cooed softly to her, trying not to imagine the images assaulting her tired mind.

He rubbed his forehead with the hand that was not holding Delilah's and felt his sorrow mix with rage.

You think too much. Isn't that what Delilah told him? *What do you feel?*

He didn't know then, but he knew now. As clear as cut crystal and just as sharp. Rage. That's what he felt. Rage that there was no one to blame, rage that answers grew more elusive, questions more dangerous. Asking why seemed to lead down dark corridors toward horrible possibilities—maybe the world is just evil, or maybe there is no reason at all, everything is simply and heartlessly random or maybe God exists and he is indifferent, cruel, even. Nowhere could he find a path toward light.

Oh yes, it was very clear what he felt. But now what?

What did he do with it now that it had a name?

"Oh, Delilah..." he whispered, not sure if he spoke for her or for himself, "I'm so sorry. Sorry I didn't know, didn't see it. I swear, if the man wasn't already dead..." He gently touched her face in slumber, the bruise on her jaw. "I know you have every right to claim you've had enough, but I'm asking you to fight one more fight. Don't let him win. I don't know if I have a right to ask... but..."

He couldn't finish. He didn't know how, didn't know what he was saying. They were just words. Words spoken to no one at all. Words he didn't know if he believed, because he didn't know what he believed anymore.

Early the next morning the nurse woke him where he'd fallen asleep in the bedside chair. "Mr. Harrison, why don't you go get something to eat?"

He woke slowly, extracting himself from the slumped, uncomfortable position in which he'd slept and rubbed his eyes. "Mm. Maybe some coffee." His gaze flicked toward Delilah who still lay sleeping.

"She'll be fine." The nurse reassured him. "I need to check a few things on her, so I'll be here. Go ahead." She smiled and gave Amos a nudge toward the door.

He walked without thinking of where he was going, his mind full of Delilah and Harold. In a fog he made his way, following color-coding on the floor: blue for x-ray, orange, cafeteria, getting a coffee to go, and in a fog, he returned, ambling like a sleepwalker back to Delilah's room. He hadn't felt so tired, so drained in longer than he could recall. Delilah's life did not seem real to him, and he couldn't imagine having the strength or the will to survive it.

He opened the door to Delilah's room slowly, not wanting to disturb her. He was surprised to find Harold on the chair by the bed crying softly as Delilah stroked his hair and whispered quietly to him. Even now it was she who reached out.

Amos stepped into the room, his boots on the floor and the click of the spring door startling Harold to his feet.

"It's okay!" Delilah said, her voice hoarse and dry. "It's okay. You know Amos. It's okay."

Harold backed away from the bed, tense and poised, his eyes wide. Wild. Unfamiliar. Filled with primal, dense fear. His lips moved rapidly in soundless words, endless repetition meant to soothe.

A soft rap on the door was followed by Sergeant Tilton peeking his head in, "Mr. Harrison?"

But he never finished, because the instant Harold saw the uniform he panicked, bolting out the door, knocking the officer backward and Amos' coffee to the floor before he disappeared down the stairwell.

"Harold!" Delilah sat up in bed, yelling after him, as the officer pulled himself together and followed Harold down the stairs.

"HAROLD!" Delilah called again, tearing the stitches in her lip. A nurse ran in, but Amos shooed her back out as he tried to calm Delilah himself.

"Ssh. C'mon, honey. It'll be okay."

"No. You don't understand. He's scared. You can't understand." She fought him with remarkable strength, adrenaline canceling the pain of her injuries.

"They only want to talk with him. That's all."

"No!"

Through the slightly open window on a current of air came shouts and the scuff of shoes on pavement in the courtyard below. Delilah tore herself free from Amos, yanking out her I.V. in the process, and stumbled to the window.

Three floors below Harold tried to fend off two hospital security guards and Sergeant Tilton by swinging his weighty backpack wildly through the air.

Amos tried to gently pull Delilah from the window, but she shook him off, and he was afraid if he were any more forceful he'd injure her further.

"Oh, God, just leave him be," Delilah muttered, tears coursing.

Harold connected with one guard in the stomach, knocking the breath out of him, and when the other tried to grab for him, Harold swung wild. The backpack arced high over his head, and slamming against the guard's temple, knocked him to the ground.

"Harold!" Delilah managed to shout out the window, and Harold whirled around.

He caught her eye and their gazes locked. Each reflected the other's pain, each desperately tried to take the other's nightmare away, wanting one another to be free. To be whole. "'Farewell! if ever fondest prayer for other's weal avail'd on high,'" he called to the sky with arms raised in offering, and even acquiescence. "'Mine will not be lost in air but waft thy name beyond the sky'! Lord..." But he could not finish. He choked on his words, his eyes filling with tears that ran unabashed down his cheeks, and he withdrew, clasping his fists against his temples, stumbling blindly in circles, tempo increasing like a dervish while a steady moan escaped from his throat.

Watching, Delilah suddenly felt it. All at once she could see what would be as clearly as she could suddenly see backward at what had been; the past rushed through her, beyond her, pointed her toward the future. And she felt it. Love. Honest, pure, pervasive. The thing she had never felt for her mother, even in her last moments, or for her father who had never meant anything to her other than fear. The thing she now realized she had merely brushed against with Virginia -- love of family, home and belonging — suddenly shot through her. As she watched Harold's fate unfold, her love for him, the honest truth of it, swelled within her. And the pain of it, the beauty. And the sudden awareness of its impending doom sucked the breath from her lungs.

Beholding heaven and feeling hell, she recalled Harold saying once when they were alone together. Only now did she understand.

Sergeant Tilton called for Harold to stop. To calm down. He held one hand out as to a wild animal, trying to appease and draw him near. But all the while, he held his gun protectively drawn. Other police cars pulled up, sirens whining down, lights flashing their garish colors. Officers jumped out, positioning themselves nearby. It incited Harold's panic and fear, fed the hysteria that sent him spinning in circles. And when Harold turned to see the guard lying unconscious on the ground -- violence by his own hand — his rage exploded. A sobbing, desperate scream finally wrenched free, "'Nothing will come of nothing'!" and he blindly charged Sergeant Tilton who called twice for him to stop.

"Stop!"

But when he didn't, the fury too powerful, the sorrow too crippling, another officer fired, knocking

Harold back two steps (One. Two.) before he fell to the ground.

"NO!" It was all Amos could do to quiet Delilah's horrific, deafening screams and to keep her from leaping out the window to save the life of the one who had saved her own. She beat her fist against the window as she screamed, knocking her cast against the sill. She kicked her legs at the air when Amos lifted her, hysteria increasing her strength—a wild animal enraged at the hunters, the trappers, the evil that had driven them all mad with desperation. He turned her toward him, trying to anchor her in his gaze, and in her panicked, stricken eyes he saw the whole world was on fire, and no one would escape alive. It terrified him.

Two nurses rushed in, and with Amos' help, they held her still long enough to inject a dose of sedative and get her into bed. Delilah fought hard, still struggling to scream even as the medication reduced her voice to a whisper. A whimper. Silence.

Jesus, God, Amos thought, half a bewildered laugh escaping through disbelieving sobs.

He turned toward the window, his hands propped against the frame. Orderlies and doctors rushed toward Harold, pushing past the guard and other police, a mad tumult of hopeless attempts at resuscitating his lifeless body. He was dead.

Dead.

In Amos, laughter and tears wound fully together, the sound of each indistinguishable from the other as defeat replaced rage, the insanity of it pushing him toward mania. He wanted to scream, to crumble, to run, but found himself unable to do anything at all.

"Let this be a dream" he whispered to no one. "Let this all be one, long, horrible dream.

Time seemed to change after that for Amos. Days bled together in a mindless blur. He closed the store and spent most of his time at the hospital, seeing the inside of his house only for a quick change of clothes. During a few quiet moments, he flashed on passing Millie or Sarah on the street but couldn't recall what was said or what he replied. They were just fuzzy images lost within the whirling emotions inside him.

All he could focus on was Delilah.

He did attend Harold's funeral, arranging to have him buried beside Virginia, but when he was asked to say a few words he could only wave his hand no and turn away. There were no words. And while he was glad to see so many people in attendance –– something that would never have happened before Delilah's influence –– he was heartbroken that the one person who should attend, needed to attend, couldn't.

Amos spent the rest of his time at the hospital, barraging doctors and nurses with questions, talking to Delilah in the hope she was still listening, talking to himself to keep from going insane at the turn they'd all taken.

Since the shooting and the surreal chaos of blood and screaming and death, Delilah hadn't moved. Not even to eat. She lay there motionless, her eyes open and unseeing, almost as though she had taken Harold into herself.

The doctors called it shock.

Amos called it a broken spirit. A soul can only take so much, and for one so young Delilah was already living on borrowed hope and faith when she first arrived. It had only been a matter of time. In fact, the moment of her implosion, as Amos referred to it, had not really surprised him, not once all the pieces came together. He saw it now.

He saw quite a lot.

The doctors said it left her in a state completely unaware of the world around her.

Amos felt it was more likely she knew, but just didn't care. And why should she?

In his mind Amos saw images of Delilah, a movie montage of Delilah in a peach straw hat leaning on his counter, of her watching fireworks or feeding the swans; and all of the images contrasted so sharply with the girl on the bed, surrounded by defeated shadows and withdrawn from any touch of life, that he thought, perhaps, he was witness to the most insane form of injustice in the world—the theft of a soul.

"Please hang on, Delilah. I can't think of one good reason why I have a right to ask you, but I'm asking anyway. And if you need a reason, make me it. I need you around. I need you to wake me up at ungodly hours of the morning to look at swans. I need you to show me what an ass I can be."

He pulled a tissue from the box on the nightstand and wiped a tear that leaked from the corner of Delilah's eye.

"Oh, man, this wasn't how it was supposed to go.," he whispered to her and held her hand. "This isn't what I imagined."

Not for Delilah.

Not like this.

Not for any of them.

Leaving his seat he turned to the window to stare down into the courtyard, suddenly realizing all the things he had envisioned Delilah doing with her life. "You know what I imagined? I imagined you with children all around you, a life full of laughter. I imagined you living in Virginia's house and leaving it to your own children. I imagined having that infectious spirit of yours in my life for a long, long time."

The empty path below wound silently through the arms of draping willow trees and sculptured flower gardens. Ordered. Planned. A place for everything and everything in its place.

"Of course, I saw Ellen doing so much more as well. I suppose I should learn life isn't always what you think it should be."

The nurse came in to change Delilah's IV bag. Amos turned toward her.

"Do you think she can hear me when I talk to her?"

The nurse glanced at Delilah, then turned to Amos. She smiled. "I think, actually, that in a way she can. Maybe not the words themselves, but the meaning gets through. The feeling. You know?"

Amos breathed deeply. The nurse was young. Compassionate. He appreciated that even though he wasn't sure he believed her.

"Mr. Harrison," the nurse continued, "you need to get some rest. She needs you to be strong for her."

Amos imagined what the nurse saw when she looked at him. He hadn't been eating or sleeping, his head felt like it was full of rocks, and he had a week's worth of beard on his face. He forced a smile. "I'm okay. A little tired maybe, but I'll be fine."

"You won't do her any good if you end up checking in here as well."

"I know, really. Thank you. I look worse than I feel."

The nurse stood a moment and smiled. "Just take care of yourself."

He nodded as she finished her work and quietly left the room.

He turned back toward the window, and as the breeze ruffled the willow branches he thought he caught a brief glimpse of two figures paused beneath the tree, dappled in patches of golden sunlight, their gazes turned up toward the window. He only saw them for a moment, but he swore it was Ellen and Virginia—full of smiles and warmth, laughter and love.

He thought of all the things he had envisioned for himself.

All that had come and gone.

When the wind changed, blowing the tangle of branches again, all he saw were dappled shadows and speckled sunlight.

Rubbing the bridge of his nose he turned back to Delilah. She lay as quiet as ever, still and unmoving.

Perhaps he imagined it.

Perhaps the nurse was right and he was hallucinating.

Perhaps he was tired and scared and alone.

Whatever gets you through the day, Amos. And although by the time he realized he heard it, he was already no longer sure of it, he did know it sounded different somehow.

He laughed. Not an ironic, bittersweet chuckle, but rather an honest, simple laugh.

An idea began to form, born of bits of old conversations, scattered words, advice ignored, lost and forgotten beliefs all drifting toward one another to form one, cohesive thought.

His continuing sorrow over Ellen was simply one last, desperate attempt at holding her near.

He rubbed his forehead and tried to clamp down on the thoughts.

To relinquish the sorrow, to take the next step toward healing meant letting her go—and if he let her go, if he willingly let loose his grasp... what? What was it? What was the next part of the equation? If he was able to willingly let her go...*didn't that mean he never really loved her*?

He held his breath as the realization sank in.

"Whatever gets you through the day." He heard the phrase in his own voice this time and heard it for what it really was: an admonition. Ellen used to lovingly point out that he was occasionally a silly man who used the oddest things as a means of comfort.

262

"Oh, Ellen. I think I understand."

He saw that if he loved her, he would be as kind to himself as she would have been, and that meant letting go the torture of sorrow and setting both himself and Ellen free.

Free.

Something inside him shifted and suddenly an image coalesced in his mind—Delilah as an older woman, crow's feet like rays of sunshine around her eyes, soft strands of greying hair falling across her shoulders in easy ringlets. She stood in a yard of emerald grass, laughing and tending roses all scarlet and yellow and pink, while a peach sunhat filtered afternoon autumn light that trickled through trees stained with the color of raging sunsets, and a flock of blinding white swans drummed the air in their angelic flight overhead...

"Delilah..." He wanted to share the thoughts tumbling through him, solidify them.

He glanced to Delilah to find her shining green eyes awaiting him. Watching. Still silently and from a distance. But watching. Encouraging.

Seeing?

Again he laughed, fuller this time, the sound mixing with tears as his memory of Ellen settled in around his heart full of warmth and comfort, and only a tiny bit of sadness.

Settling into the chair he rubbed his eyes and studied his hands. "I'm an idiot, aren't I? Always making things more difficult than they have to be." Before him lay a girl who had been through more in her short life than he'd ever experience, even if he lived to be one hundred. And she survived.

Is it that simple?

Do you simply *choose* to survive? To live?

Is that what Delilah had been saying all along?

Whatever gets you through the day. It meant something different now.

"I understand now, I think," he whispered.

"'We have been friends together in sunshine and in shadow.' Caroline E.S. Norton."

He looked up, almost certain he heard Delilah speak, but so full of ghosts and private thoughts he didn't know whether the quiet voice came from inside or out.

As he stood and stepped toward her, her eyes followed him and seemed to dance with a silent, distant laughter.

"Delilah?"

Perhaps he had imagined it.

Delilah.

But then he remembered -- like a sudden summer storm, or an easy evening breeze, or dreams that feel like memories, he remembered...

You never could tell with Delilah.

That was the thing with her.

You never could tell.

You never could tell with Delilah.

57825138R00163

Made in the USA
Charleston, SC
23 June 2016